MED̶ ̶̶ ̶̶̶

AND MAYHEM

BY

S R WATERMEYER

SABGE Publishing Ltd
ISBN-13: 978-1-9161755-2-5

To the fabulous and selfless colleagues and friends in the NHS who look after and care for the sick, old, demented, bereaved, worried, and traumatised members of society. They see life as it really is and give their all and more for our patients every day of their working lives. Amidst both suffering and joy, they still manage to have a laugh, for humour is surely one of the best medicines.

CONTENTS

ACKNOWLEDGMENTS

To my soulmate Ali, who has put up with me for nearly a quarter of a century and is still the love of my life (soppy bastard that I am).

CHAPTER 1

It was 0730 a.m. and gentle snoring emanated from the upstairs bedroom of a two-up, two-down terrace house in the Welsh Capital of Cardiff. Dr Rick Donovan, Senior Registrar in Obstetrics and Gynaecology, lay comatose in his bed and unbeknown to him, he was not alone. Two weeks previously he had invested in a heavy duty alarm clock with a massive, bloody great speaker; this was in view of his propensity for ignoring the easy-going alarm of his mobile phone and returning to the land of nod. Rick jolted to a semi-conscious state and cursed as the electronic gadget thundered out its wake up call designed to raise Lazarus from his two thousand year kip, let alone gently awaken a mortal from his slumber. The medic moaned audibly as he shifted his weary body to enable his outstretched hand to fumble over the switches of his new alarm clock in order to turn the bugger of modern gadgetry well and truly off. However, the only button his searching fingers found was the volume control, and inevitably any relief he sought from his attempts to turn off the wretched contraption, only succeeded in increasing the oscillating bleeps to a deafening crescendo. Such was the din, that the dog next door started to howl and Rick's increasingly aroused state was further heightened by the irate ranting of Miss Enid Jones, his somewhat religious and extremely vocal, next door neighbour. Rick had learnt that Miss Jones was a formidable woman, both in stature and personality and most certainly was not one to be trifled with. The cacophony from his cursed alarm clock continued unabated until Rick managed to trace the lead to a somewhat disintegrated wall socket into which the alarm's plug was precariously inserted. With his eyes still closed, he pulled furiously on the plug and to his relief, the booming beeps abated, but only after Rick had received a retaliatory electric shock that was equally effective in completing his startled awakening.

If the sound of the alarm clock hadn't succeeded in annoying Miss Jones, the echo of Rick's uncensored, "Bugger, bugger, B-U-G-G-E-R!" through the thin wall of their little terrace houses really did – it was another affront to her social and religious dignities. She roared through the not-so–

thick adjoining brick wall some fervent abuse that Rick was damned and destined to spend the entirety of his afterlife in Hell's burning fires. For Rick, the influence of the previous night's ten pints of Best Bitter impressed upon him that he was probably already in hell, and that for once the old biddy who was his neighbour, was doubtless correct in her assumptions. The provision of a brief stint of silence from Rick did eventually calm the situation. However, his horrendous hangover was going to need several pints of water, a packet of paracetamol and twenty four hours which he did not have. When eventually Miss Jones's ranting and raving about Rick's blasphemous and ungodly ways ceased, and her runt of a dog, Molly, whose high pitched howling had accompanied his mistress's histrionics, had finally quietened down, Rick thought about getting up. But with the alarm clock disconnected and the neighbourhood reasonably peaceful again, Rick snuggled down under his duvet. The intention of giving himself just another five, wonderful minutes in his pit in order to gather his thoughts was too much to resist. This proved to be unfortunate since far from gathering his thoughts with the intention of aiding his ability to rise from his bed, he predictably drifted back to sleep.

It was over an hour later that once more he stirred to the sound of another gadget, this time the persistent ringing from his mobile phone. He clumsily picked up the device resting on his bedside table and grunted some unintelligible vocalism. The reply he received sobered him up.

"Rick, this is Rachel, your senior house officer. Forgive my French, but where the hell are you? We've started the old man's operating list, and the first case is a vaginal hysterectomy and none of us can do it except you or the boss. He is not going to be pleased Rick, to find that his senior registrar can't even be bothered to turn up for his operating list. You're in deep shit and unless you get that lazy butt out of bed and get down here in the next ten minutes, you're without doubt, dead meat."

"Oh shit! Oh bollocks! Rachel hold on, give me ten minutes, I'll be there. For God's sake don't start without me."

As Rick bounced out of bed with a new found energy, he suddenly and with a degree of shock noticed that he was not alone. As he looked down on his double bed and noticed the outline of a slim human form under his duvet. There was the unmistakeable gentle sound of shallow breathing, almost purring and then movement. A small female foot adorned with beautifully manicured nails protruded from under the bedclothes, followed by a more than pleasing shapely ankle and knee, and finally a silky naked thigh. It was then that it all came back to him. The nightclub, the booze, the pretty girl, but what the hell was her name? A slim arm reached out and grabbed him, pulling him back down onto the bed and he felt his loins stir. Before he knew it he was on the receiving end of a rather pleasant snog and he succumbed to the inevitable.

"Darling we will have to make it quick. I should have been in the operating theatre five minutes ago!"

"I'll give you the best five minutes of your life," she purred and with that Dr Rick Donovan was more than happy to dispense his duty. Five minutes later the deed was done and fortunately all sides were satisfied. The young lady concerned turned over and snuggled back down into the duvet, with instructions from Rick to help herself to breakfast and leave at a time of her choosing. However, Rick was, by now, later than late.

The sound of passionate lovemaking did not go unnoticed by Miss Jones's highly perceptive sense of hearing and immediately she was bellowing through the wall further accounts of Rick's impending doom on account of his irreligious acts. Molly, who followed avidly in her mistress's footsteps, was not to be outdone, and the grisly howls started up once more. Such pandemonium was now totally ignored by Rick, who concentrated all his efforts into washing, dressing, and driving to the hospital in record time. His boss, Sir John Rawarse, was not a man to displease. The fact that he was known to be a complete bastard to all his juniors even when they behaved in a competent and professional manner was worrying. What fate awaited Rick if Rawarse discovered that his newly appointed senior registrar had missed an operating list because of a hangover and a spot of nookie was too awful to contemplate, although admittedly Rawarse was unlikely to find out about the latter.

Running out of his house, the young gynaecologist clambered into his brand new and most prized possession, a gleaming British racing green *Mini Cooper S* that he had bought straight from the showroom just a few weeks earlier. His new motor was in stark contrast to Enid's old beat up *Austin Mini* parked directly outside her front door. Rick turned the key and the powerful engine burst into life. After an interesting drive to work with at least one flash from a speed camera, Rick screeched into the hospital car park. He charged up several flights of stairs and into the operating theatre's changing rooms where he rapidly got into his theatre blues and stumbled into the operating theatre. His hair was bedraggled, his heart racing and the faint smell of *Brains* best bitter formed an aurora around him. The patient was already anaesthetised, her legs in stirrups, and an officious looking theatre sister was tapping her fingers impatiently on the instrument tray. Rick rapidly scrubbed up and then donned an operating gown over the top of his theatre blues. A team of junior doctors was gathered around the patient's bottom end. They all looked suitably relieved to see Rick and had evidently been waiting for him. He nodded an acknowledgement to his colleagues before greeting them formally. "Morning team, are we all well this morning?"

"Streuth Rick you look rough as a badger's arse!" Rachel was never one to be short of compliments.

"Rachel, how delightful to see you." Rick feigned a forced smile. "Please do us and the rest of the country a favour - never contemplate a job in the diplomatic corps, will you?"

Rick's gaze diverted from Rachel's more than

pleasant facial features towards the gowned and prepared patient. What greeted him did nothing to quell his ailing disposition. To be faced with anybody's tail end sticking out from under a set of sterile theatre sheets first thing in the morning was hardly the best way to start anyone's day. With every passing month, the anticipated romance of being a doctor was further dashed and the rose tinted spectacles through which Rick had previously viewed the medical profession was slipping away. Bowel surgeons knee deep in shit, bladder surgeons covered in wee, gynaecologists painting a metaphorical hall through a metaphorical letter box, and pathologists spending more time with stiff, dead people than they did with their own wives was hardly the stuff of "living the dream". The added sleep deprivation from stressful on-calls, and constantly dealing with death, disease and suffering was hardly a selling point for recruitment.

Rick often thought at times like this, why on earth he had chosen gynaecology as a profession. He could have made a reasonably good lawyer, or perhaps an accountant or indeed he could have gone for a job in the city where he could have made millions for doing not a lot. 'But no, instead here I am between this enormous woman's thighs taking out a diseased womb with its associated blood and bodily secretions.' However, the truth of it was, was that there was nothing that compared with the feeling of satisfaction in helping and often curing patients with life altering diseases. At times, complaints and criticism from disgruntled patients and their relatives was soul destroying, but in the main Joe public was very grateful and appreciative of the medics and nurses who really cared. And Rick really cared.

As the young gynaecologist seated himself between the good lady's thighs, he could hear Sir John Rawarse chatting to a colleague in the corridor just outside the operating theatre. There was no mistaking Sir John's pucker English accent which was not always well received in the Welsh heartland. He had a formidable reputation, to say the least, and as such the senior consultant he did not tolerate fools, inefficiency, with the worst sin of all being lack of punctuality.

Rick muttered to himself as he faced the unfortunate woman's fanny. He nodded to the theatre sister, indicating that he required the scalpel, and prompted by the proximity of his consultant boss got on making the first incision. The knife sliced neatly through the flesh of his patient and Rick expertly clamped, cut and then sutured off blood vessels and ligaments as he worked skilfully towards excising the patient's womb and delivering it through her vaginal opening. All went according to plan until the young surgeon started to suture and close the top of the patient's birth canal, when out of the blue, pandemonium broke out at the good lady's top end. There was clearly something irritating the patient's airway and the red faced, sparsely bearded anaesthetist appeared powerless to sort it out. The result was that the enormous unconscious lady started to involuntarily cough. Great spasms ricocheted down her abdomen heaving and pushing her fat and voluminous bowel and squirming intestines out of her front end and directly into Rick's unsuspecting lap. The more Rick tried to stuff the writhing mass back into the patient's front aperture, the more they insisted on spilling out. This unfortunate misadventure was timed to perfection to coincide with Sir John's arrival in the operating theatre.

"D-o-n-o-v-a-n! What the hell are you doing? If I wanted this patient to have her guts surgically removed, I would have asked the bowel surgeons. Now kindly replace her intestines before I wrap them around your bloody neck!" Rawarse bellowed from the operating theatre entrance.

But as hard as Rick tried to replace the squirming,

slimy loops of bowel, the more the patient coughed and so yet more bowel was deposited on his lap, until half the contents of the portly patients innards had been evacuated through her open front passage. The young gynaecologist was not having a good day. It didn't help that he was still recovering from the effects of the previous night's booze and to experience a sea of slithering colon emerging from the unfortunate patient's fanny did nothing to help the situation. Rick pleaded with the anaesthetist and prayed to the Good Lord.

The young gynaecologist prayers must have been heard, for God did not abandon him. The good lady patient ceased her unconscious retching, as the anaesthetist crossed himself in gratitude and Rick slowly and painstakingly started to replace her extruding bowel, thanking God as he did so. Sir John Rawarse, appeared to be at least momentarily silenced. But it was not to last. The manual handling of the patient's bowel increased her propensity for flatulence and Rick's intimacy with the patient's bodily functions took a step closer as she loudly let rip from her hefty backside.

With scorched nostrils, the young gynaecologist swore under his breath, then surreptitiously had a sneaky look around to ensure that he had not been overheard. It appeared that the coast was clear since Rawarse seemed to have exited. Rick inserted and tied the final suture, completing the operation and in doing so released a wary sigh of relief. The patient was well, the surgery was sorted and he had got off lightly with regard to Rawarse's legendary temper.

However, Sir John far from exiting that operating theatre, had silently positioned himself immediately behind a surgical stack system just out of Rick's peripheral visual field, but well within hearing distance of anything his young apprentice cared to speak about. The Theatre Sister, who had been around long enough to know Sir John's antics glared warily at Rick, her eyes darting behind her in a vain attempt to warn Rick of the old man's presence. But it was to no avail.

The naivety of youth caused the theatre staff to quake in their operating shoes as Rick voiced his unguarded and unwise comments,"Ahhh....Thank God that's done, and I cannot believe that the old Bastard makes his exit just before I complete the surgery. He really is a miserable old sod, don't you think so Sister?"

There followed an eerie silence.

"Oh come Sis, I know the patients like him, but

sometimes he is a miserable old git, don't you think?"

A death like atmosphere pervaded the operating theatre, and Rick finally started to realise that something was very wrong. He experienced a sudden sense of foreboding. Then, to one side of the operating theatre Sir John Rawarse reappeared. The senior consultant looked down on the miserable specimen before him as if he had been dragged straight from the gutter. As Rick glanced up at his boss, he saw the redness of unadulterated rage rise up the man's neck and fill his gaunt cheeks with uncharacteristic colour. Rawarse was quivering with such fury that he was unable to vent his feelings of wrath by his usual shouting episodes that could be heard on the other side of the hospital. Instead, as his lips moved and he tried to vocalise, a single squeak emanated from his usually masterful voice box and the rage within him doubled to a crescendo of murderous proportions.

As the old man's blood pressure rocketed to newly found heights on account of the heinous behaviour of his senior registrar, Rawarse felt suddenly light-headed and faint. His heart began to thump so fast it felt like it would burst from his chest, and then the pain, by God the pain, it was almost unbearable. The world started to swirl around him and he started to feel nauseated. Then without any warning to his trembling colleagues, Rawarse collapsed, gurgling abuse at his senior registrar as he hit the floor at the entrance to his own operating theatre.

The theatre staff were stunned. They each stared in disbelief as the old man collapsed in front of them. For a few seconds no one moved, frightened that at any moment this, their senior surgeon would suddenly sit up and bellow chastisement at each of them. Perhaps it was some sort of joke. After all, Rawarse had not had a day off sick in twenty years. Was it possible that the man that they all feared for so long was popping his clogs here in front of them in his own operating theatre?

Rick, despite his delicate state, was the first to move. After the initial shock of it all, he more than anyone realised the seriousness of the situation that confronted them. With adrenaline now pumping through his body, he rushed over to where Rawarse lay and, shaking him, tried in vain to rouse him. It was no good. Rick felt the old man's pulse then listened for any sign of breathing.

'Shit! Nothing!' Rick vocalised. 'The old bastard's arrested.' He tore off his operating gloves and surgical mask and got to work on his boss, who was by now starting to go blue. "Somebody, call the crash team. Yes, you, now and bloody well get a move on," Rick bellowed at one of the theatre technicians. "Rachel, get an IV line in and fetch me the emergency drugs. Where's the sodding anaesthetist pissed off to, somebody, anybody, get him in here now."

By the time the crash team arrived Rick had not only intubated but also defibrillated Rawarse. His ailing boss was starting to look somewhat better. Colour had returned to his cheeks as his heart started to beat once again and Rick, content that the old man was at least going to live for the time being, let the crash team take over his care. Sir John Rawarse was whisked off to the Coronary Care Unit (CCU), but only after the senior anaesthetist of the crash team congratulated Rick on saving the his boss's life.

The theatre staff, including Rachel, who had been assisting him, were impressed by Rick's leadership qualities, as well as his surgical skills. Despite the fact that he was a cocky sod, he had completed a very difficult hysterectomy and then had been the only one to react with promptness to Sir John's collapse. The staff's unspoken admiration and confidence in him seemed to mature him. The remaining three cases on the operating list were carried out uneventfully and efficiently. At the end of the morning, Rick was thankful the list was finished. He thanked the theatre staff and, having showered and changed, made his way to the ward to review his patients.

The afternoon clinic proceeded reasonably well and the forty patients that needed to be seen were dealt with smoothly and efficiently, but perhaps not given quite enough time to allow for the empathy and satisfactory explanation they deserved. But this was a theme throughout the beleaguered NHS – too many patients, not enough staff. Towards the end of his busy day Rick started to tire, but his conscience dictated that he should visit Rawarse on the Coronary Care Unit, even if it was just to see that his grumpy boss was still alive. No one offered to accompany him. Although they respected him, no one much liked the boss.

On arrival at the CCU, Rick heard the unmistakable voice of John Rawarse bellowing across the room at some poor student nurse who evidently failed to live up to his expectations. Rick smiled to himself. Not even a cardiac arrest could dampen the old man's vocal protestations, although on seeing his senior registrar walking towards him he became strangely subdued. 'The quiet before the storm,' Rick thought as he braced himself.

"Hello, Sir." He feigned his best smile.

Rawarse looked him up and down contemptuously.

CHAPTER 2

Belinda Jones arrived home after a hard day's work at the bank. In fact it had been more than a hard day, it had been an exceptionally traumatic day. In addition, she was unusually tired and slightly irritated at the nagging discomfort in her pelvis. She had not been on top of the world for the last few days, but told herself that these minor medical ailments were sent to try one, and most of the time had an uncanny knack of clearing up spontaneously. She closed her front door, walked somewhat uncomfortably into her lounge and collapsed on her settee in front of a goldfish bowl. Charlie, her solitary aquatic companion swam round and round in circles, until Belinda sprinkled fish food onto the surface of the water which was duly gulped up by a grateful Charlie, who was then subjected to a full and traumatic description of his Mistress's day. For a goldfish, Charlie was not a bad listener and at least he didn't answer back.

Belinda found herself saying sorry to her brainless confidant for the unforgiving and rather prolonged rant she had exposed him to. Apologies complete, she exited the lounge to run herself a long, hot bubble bath before taking pleasure in immersing herself in the soft fragrant bubbles that soothed her aching body. As Belinda lay relaxed in her watery haven, so too did she really start to unwind and reflect on some of the upsetting events of the day. Firstly, she had had an unfortunate row with her manager, a wiry old character called Sidney Blithe. The wrinkly old man, who was mature enough to be her grandfather, had asked her out on a date. Belinda had firmly but politely declined. Later on in the morning, she had caught him standing over her, looking down her blouse and ogling at her breasts, the lecherous old git. When she had again made it perfectly plain that she was uninterested in his pervy attention, by telling him in no uncertain terms to 'piss off', a heated argument started, the result of which was likely to result in any potential promotion being delayed.

The second trauma of the day was the discovery that her dashing fiancé, Rupert Daventry, had been having a torrid affair with Tracey Buxome. Tracey was one of the new bank clerk apprentices, although as far as Belinda was concerned she would be better off on a dairy farm, where once appropriately impregnated her potential yield would far outstrip even the most productive of Jersey cows. Certainly, she lived up to her name - what she lacked in grey matter she more than made up for in breast development.

The trouble was, Belinda had thought she was deeply in love with Rupert Daventry after meeting him at a Banker's Christian Association encounter two years previously. He was tall, handsome and athletic, and professed to be a man of principle. Prayer meetings often finished with a round of hugs and Rupert had an amazing knack of being in the right place at the right time for hugging her, almost to the exclusion of every other person in the room. This was all rather embarrassing, yet in a strange way she could not help but enjoy the attention and the flattery of a member of the opposite sex. The hugs had progressed to a post prayer-meeting orange juice and then eventually the two of them had become an item. Belinda, although mature in many ways, was still hopelessly naïve with regard to sex. She had been brought up within the strict moral and religious confines of a convent and therefore had very little experience of the male gender. Rupert Daventry, on the other hand, was a wolf in sheep's clothing - a flatterer, a cad, and a sex maniac. In private male company he would jest that the females who attended the Banker's Christian Association put together were less desirable than the ugliest of warthogs and not worth even a rudimentary poke, except of course Belinda, who was exceptionally beautiful and who he, Rupert Daventry intended to bed - another notch on an increasingly scarred bed post.

Belinda for her part, had not suspected for one moment that Rupert's intentions were dishonourable and she had absolutely no inkling that he was a complete bastard. She was in love and on the highest of romantic highs. For Rupert, Belinda Jones was the ultimate challenge, a beautiful, untouched, highly principled, yet naïve conquest. The cad had had to work hard to get what he wanted and even went as far as organising a transfer to work at the same branch.

After sleeping with the head of personnel, which thereafter necessitated a quick trip to the local clap clinic, to burn off an unsightly wart, Rupert managed to secure a desk next to Belinda on the second floor of the bank. He feigned complete shock that she was now his colleague "on the desk next door" and convinced her that fate must have played a part in bringing them together. Thereafter the rascal took full advantage of her romantic inclinations, wined and dined her, showered her with flowers and roses of every conceivable size, shape and colour, professed his undying and everlasting love for her and finally precipitously asked for her hand in marriage. Belinda, despite warnings from some of her more worldly-wise colleagues, failed to see the shit for what he was, and promptly accepted the bastard's hand in marriage. But fortunately, the nuptials never took place.

Belinda stirred back to the present and again felt a twinge of sharp pain in her pelvis. She submerged herself further under the soothing bubble bath suds and her thoughts once again wondered.

The nuptials had been set for later that year and Belinda had so looked forward to a wonderful white, fairy tale wedding. She had been so happy and so in love, she would have done anything for him. Yet she now despised herself for allowing him to ply her with alcohol, which she was hopelessly sensitive too, and take her virginity in a frenzy of lust veiled in his bogus love for her. The whole sorry episode had taken place some six weeks previously. In truth and much to her dismay, she couldn't even describe it as, a pleasant experience. A couple of thrusts and it was all over. Certainly, Belinda had not allowed a repetition of such events to occur and Rupert had been informed that he would have to wait until they were husband

and wife before any further physical intimacy took place. It was her only hope that any future intimacy lasted longer than a few seconds.

The discovery that very afternoon that her by-now ex-fiancée had rogered Miss Buxome was initially a bit of a shock. However, on further reflection Belinda had experienced one or two doubts over the last few weeks about marrying the cad. The fact that now he'd been caught red-handed - or should she say red-faced - with his underpants around his ankles whilst Miss Buxome writhed beneath him on the manager's desk, was in some ways rather fortuitous. Apparently, Mr Sidney Blithe, their not-so-proper nor prudish manager, had strolled into his office and been justly irritated that his desk with its array of important documents was being used as a shagging couch. Sidney had walked in on the couple precisely at the point of Rupert's orgasm. A reliable witness had informed Belinda that Mr Blithe had quite rightly contradicted Rupert's groans of, "Yes, Yes, Yes!" with a repudiated, "No, No, No, Mr Daventry, that will not do at all."

Miss Buxome, whose writhing around had by now ceased more because of Rupert's prematurity and the flaccid state of his member than because the couple had been inadvertently discovered, had been equally hacked off. She had concurred with Mr Blithe's appraisal of the situation by repeating, "No, No, No Mr Daventry, that will not do at all."

In one fell swoop Rupert Daventry had lost his job, his fiancé, and his credibility as a lover, and as far as Belinda was concerned it served the bastard right. Her eyes had finally been opened. Mr Blithe, on the other hand, had suffered the destruction of some important paperwork that had been sitting on his desk at the time of the copulation. Furthermore he was now due to suffer the indignity of explaining to his own boss how such important documents came to be in such a state. For her part in the proceedings, Miss Buxome had been severely reprimanded but narrowly managed to avoid losing her job by agreeing to put in some unpaid overtime. Mr Blithe had undoubtedly spied her fine assets and would make the most of her agreed, after-work tasks. The odd thing was that Mr Blithe had instructed the nubile apprentice that the paper work for such tasks was unfortunately located at his house, so Tracey would have to meet him there later. It was known that Blithe was close to retirement and also assumed that the old boy wanted to go out with a bang. Miss Buxome was apparently only too pleased to comply.

In her bath suds, Belinda pondered that at least

she had rumbled the truth about Rupert before marrying him. She would now be spared such infidelities within the matrimonial state when potential children were around to be hurt. Miss Jones had learnt more about the darker side of human nature in that one day than in all the preceding ten years. She surprised herself by muttering, "Men, they are all bastards, guided more by their dicks than their brains." Yet still within her she longed for a lifetime partner, a man she could truly love and trust.

She sank deeper into the comfort of her bubble bath and dreamt of such a man. Then it happened again, only this time it was more than just a nagging sensation. An excruciating twinge shot through her pelvis and doubled her up in pain. Belinda, not accustomed to swearing of any kind on account of her strict religious upbringing, surprised herself by mouthing, 'Oh shit that's sore.'

She sat up abruptly, spilling the foamy bath water over the side as she did so. Her hand clutched at her abdomen on the right side as a wave of pain pierced through her like a knife. Then, much to her relief, it disappeared as fast as it came, but she felt strangely nauseated and, oddly, her shoulder ached. Belinda consoled herself with the fact that all this was probably secondary to stress. Certainly it had been a traumatic day. She lay in the bath for another ten minutes before rising from the warm, aromatic water, and as she did so she felt strangely weak. Then something rather unexpected happened. As Belinda dried her nether regions, she noticed a red stain on the starched white towel. "God, I'm bleeding." She frowned to herself. This completely unexpected scenario forced her to recall the timing of her last period. In the commotion and whirlwind of the events of the last month she had failed to notice that her period was in fact two weeks late. She immediately thought back to the night when she had allowed Rupert to take advantage. Belinda did not remember taking any precautions in her inebriated state and she was positive that Rupert had neither the inclination nor the self-control to don a Durex during the unfortunate debacle. Belinda trembled with fear, firstly at the possibility of pregnancy and the fact that she might be miscarrying, and secondly at the social stigma of being unmarried. What would her religious friends say?

Belinda finished drying herself off, put on a flowery pair of pyjamas that her great Aunt had given her for Christmas and exited the bathroom. Trying to take her mind off her late period and bleeding, she busied herself around her flat, tidying up a few bits and pieces, and then concocted a tuna pasta dish, together with a cup of tea. Half an hour or so later she had calmed down, having adopted a philosophical approach to her predicament of 'what will be, will be.' In reality she was a person with a stoical nature and stable temperament. Belinda decided that if the pain in her abdomen became constant in nature or unbearable she would of course, be forced to telephone the doctor. Since it was at present neither of these and her little bit of bleeding had settled, there was no point in bothering anyone yet. No, she didn't want to disturb anyone tonight – but she would go for a check-up first thing in the morning.

The young woman couldn't finish eating her supper, for in truth she was not terribly hungry. She snuggled up on her sofa listening to Vivaldi's Four Seasons before drifting off to sleep. It was about ten o'clock when she awoke and she did so with a start. Her flowery pyjamas and dressing gown were soaked in blood. She could feel the loss coming from her and realised that she was haemorrhaging and haemorrhaging badly. On trying to get up from the sofa, she felt suddenly drained and devoid of all energy. She could feel her heart racing and knew that something was terribly wrong. The sight of copious quantities of one's own blood is enough to make anyone panic; yet Belinda remained calm, though she was now convinced of the need to urgently seek help. Pain gripped her once again and she muttered to herself, "Help, I must call for help."

A sense of alarm now started to grip her. She looked around the room for the cordless telephone and remembered she left it in the bedroom. The walls around her started to sway and her vision became blurred. Belinda forced herself up and out of the sofa and as she did so there was a gush of blood that rushed from between her legs. Unsteadily she held onto one arm of the sofa and vomited, becoming disorientated and unbalanced as she did so, and then, by God, the pain increased. She felt as if someone had opened up her insides and were gouging away at her innards. The young woman collapsed onto the floor and rolled up into ball holding her abdomen as if in some way this would ease her suffering. She felt weak and drained and sick. By now mild panic had turned full swing into unadulterated terror. She knew she was losing blood fast and she knew that there was something terribly wrong going on inside of her. "I must get to the phone," she whispered to herself. Belinda crawled laboriously inch by inch towards the bedroom door and the telephone which she knew was now her only salvation. Her flat was on the first floor of an apartment block and the entry buzzer sounded. She tried to shout, but it was hopeless. They would never hear her from the street outside and she would never make it to the intercom system in time for whoever it was to hear her pleas for help. Belinda continued to struggle towards the only possible means of rescue, but her attempts to move forward became slower and more arduous. She was barely conscious as her hand reached up onto the bedside table and pulled the phone down onto the floor beside her. Through blurred vision she forced her fingers to press 999.

The operator's voice seemed somehow alien and distant as if she wasn't real at all, but just a figment of Belinda's hazy consciousness. "Hello, which emergency service do you require? Hello, hello, is anybody there?"

"Help me please," Belinda whispered so softly it was barely audible.

The worried and empathetic voice of the operator repeated, "Do you need the police?"

"No, ambulance." With a huge effort of pure will Belinda managed to whisper the beginning of her address before a cloud seemed to float across her mind dampening her conscious state. She felt strangely light-headed and the fainter she became, so the more the pain eased. She was distantly aware that she was losing more blood from between her legs but now it seemed not to matter.

She dropped the telephone that echoed with the frantic words of the operator. "Hello, hello, hello? Please answer me... answer me please, an ambulance is on its way, hold on, we'll be with you soon."

Belinda entered a state of the most unusual tranquillity. Despite the traumatic events of that day and evening, together with her own realisation that she could possibly be on the way to an undignified exit from this world, she was so peaceful now, so unafraid. Euphoria seemed to take over her oxygen-starved brain. She saw only a beautiful and welcoming light drawing her closer in. This blissful state was interrupted only briefly as she thought for a split second of Rupert and murmured, "Bastard." She knew somehow that the light disapproved of her choice of nouns. Then there was nothing.

Paddy O'Connell and his mate Horace Finnigan were sitting in their ambulance munching their way through the greasiest and tastiest fish and chips probably in the entirety of South Wales. The radio whined and crackled before bursting into life - an urgent call and it was for them. The seriousness of the operator's voice convinced them both not to finish their gourmet meals - it appeared that this call regarding what sounded like a young woman who was barely conscious, took priority.

Horace threw his unfinished chips with abundant ketchup into the side door storage holder, wiped any residual sauce from his mouth, and frowning, turned to his paramedic mate in the adjacent seat,

"Streuth Pad, it sounds like she's a goner; better blue light it over there."

"Too friggin' right Horace, flip the switch and I'll put me friggin' foot down," Paddy replied.

The ambulance sped through the night streets of Cardiff, through red lights, amber lights and straight through crossroads, trusting a flashing blue light and the common sense of the public to either stop or slow down, but certainly to give way. As the ambulance sped through one of the more affluent areas of the city, Paddy gestured to Horace to activate the siren.

"But Pad, there ain't no cars in front of us, look mate it's a clear road." Horace looked quizzically at his friend.

"Yeah, I know but look at all them rich bastards' houses. Time to give them a late night wake up call,"

Paddy retorted with a wry grin on his middle-aged face. The ambulance hastened at full speed, lights blazing and siren at full blast, along the empty road towards where Belinda Jones lay unconscious with blood leaking into her abdomen and out of her fanny.

One of the houses that the speeding ambulance rushed past on its way to save Belinda was that of a perverted elderly bank manager. A flushed Mr Blithe was in bed with his junior bank clerk as the sound of the siren rushed by and then on into the night. Miss Buxome's ample, bare breasts heaved back and forwards in rhythm to her lovemaking to a man old enough to be her grandfather. Her eyes darted around the bedroom at the wealth on display and she pondered how long the old git would live. Her situation had turned from almost certain dismissal to early promotion, lavish presents and perhaps even a precipitous wedding. She could then only pray that Sidney would kick the bucket sooner rather than later.

Miss Buxome could hardly believe her luck. "Oh Sidney, Sidney, a real man at last," she purred into her boss's ear as she faked a well-rehearsed orgasm.

"I know my darling," Mr Sidney Blithe responded. But the smile on his face was not one of ignorant bliss, but that of a sly old fox that had just had his oats.

CHAPTER 3

It was late when Rick finally finished at the hospital and it was starting to get dark. In view of his current domestic circumstances, he was fast becoming the master of evasion. Having picked up a Chinese takeaway on the way home, he parked his car under a lamp post around the corner from his house so that he could enter his domestic quarters as inconspicuously as possible. He locked his prized *Mini Cooper S* and walking around the bend of the street, did a 180 degree turn to inspect and ensure all was in order, in particular that there was no bird shit deposited on his beloved paintwork. The young gynaecologist then literally tiptoed along, peering forward to establish that the coast was clear and that there was no sign of either Miss Enid Jones or her wretched dog. When he was sure that his neighbourly foes were not in sight, Rick made a home run for his front door. There was however, the obstacle of the front gate with its annoyingly rusty hinges to negotiate before he could safely reach the sanctuary that awaited him. He reached the gate in record time and stopped abruptly, chastising himself as he did so.

"Rick Donovan, what the hell are you doing?" It was more of a statement than a question. "This is my house, I've done nothing wrong, and I'm scared of running into a seventy-year-old woman and her mongrel," Rick murmured to himself. Yet still, as he carefully pushed the gate open, his heart sank as it creaked and moaned, almost begging for a drop of oil to lubricate its sorry hinges. Immediately there followed the noise of a dog barking from within his next door neighbour's house. It was the unmistakable snarl of that nasty little mutt, Molly, and was quickly accompanied by Miss Jones's shrieks, sounding as sharp-tongued and irritable as she had been that same morning.

Rick ran the three steps up his very short garden path to his front door and frantically pushed his key into the lock. He found himself almost panicking to get inside. He could hear Miss Jones emerging from her front entrance just as he got into his own small hall, clutching his Chinese takeaway, before swiftly and almost silently closing his own front door. Safe inside and looking up to heaven, he whispered a grateful "thank you" and then felt ridiculously stupid for behaving in such a manner. He rationalised his behaviour by concluding that he had had quite enough traumas for one day and the last thing he now needed was a show down with his highly opinionated next door neighbour. Rick went into the kitchen and poured himself a drink. As fate would have it, one of his colleagues had gone off sick that afternoon and to add insult to injury to the adverse events of his day, he had been asked to do the on-call literally as he left the hospital. Although he enjoyed nothing better than a few benders, he never drank when on-call, and so substituted his favourite beer with an alcohol-free lager. Rick settled down with his takeaway in front of the television and, having munched, slurped and chewed his way through his supper, he clambered up the stairs for a shower before climbing wearily into **bed**. By the bedside table, he noticed a piece of paper with a hastily written note thanking him for his hospitality (in more ways than one) and a telephone number. Clearly the young woman who he had entertained the night before was a decent sort. She had tidied up after herself and clearly wanted more than just a one night stand, but strangely Rick was disinclined. He relaxed under his feather duvet and weary from his stressful day, sighed to himself, "A-h-h-h, Thank God", but he did so quietly, conscious of not upsetting Miss Jones with any further audible blasphemy that her super sensitive hearing aid might pick up.

Whenever he was on call, the last thing that Rick did before falling asleep was to phone the hospital and check with his junior colleagues that there were no outstanding problems on the labour ward or on the gynaecology ward.

After a few rings, Rachel Smithers promptly answered her bleep. "Hello, Dr Rachel Smithers, on call Senior House Officer", she spoke formally, fully expecting a referral from a GP or other hospital colleague.

Rick could picture his voluptuous colleague in her theatre blues, long flowing red hair and piercing green eyes, "Hi, Rachel, it's Rick. Any problems? Anything going on? Do you need help with anything? And are you missing me?" Rick immediately regretted his rather unprofessional, "and are you missing me?"

However to his surprise, Rachel responded, "Oh yes…"

There was a moment's awkward silence before his junior colleague responded, "Oh, um, ah, actually all is relatively quiet here." Another moment's silence, then, "But …um...I am missing you."

This was all that Rick needed, "Well ma'am, I take it that means professionally everything is quiet, the patients are all safe and that you will have dinner with me on Friday?" Rick decided to strike while the iron was hot and his loins stirred at the thought of giving Rachel Smithers a damn good seeing to.

She responded, "I might, then again I might not." Rachel teased him. "But probably I will."

"Good, that's a date then." Rick was secretly very pleased with himself, he wanted to chat further to his colleague, but now was not the time. He ended the telephone call on a professional note. "Rachel, please, if you've got any problems or worries tonight don't hesitate to give me a call."

"OK, thanks boss. See you on Friday if not before." Rachel rang off. Rick settled down into his more than comfortable bed, and confident that everything was satisfactory at the hospital, fell into a deep and pleasurable sleep.

Next door, Miss Enid Jones was busy lighting candles in her front room in preparation for the late night prayer meeting that she had organised. It was meant to be a vigil for those persecuted members of the Church who had suffered great hardship under the communist regime in the old Soviet Bloc, particularly those persecuted Christians in Siberia. Enid had been particularly proud that her humble home had been chosen as the venue for such a meeting and had made all necessary preparations to ensure the event was a success. She had even borrowed a portable organ to guarantee that those members of the St Ethel Memorial choir who attended would have adequate instrumental accompaniment. Enid had expected ten or so of her devout friends to turn up and so was thrilled when her front room overflowed with a throng of about thirty evangelists, half of them choir members. In no time at all the prayer meeting was underway, some might even say, it was swinging. The vigil was initially intended to be a quiet and reflective affair. But the few serene gospel songs chosen appeared to take on a life of their own. Once they had started, the old crooners, liking the sound of their own voices, triumphantly bellowed out number after number of gospel music, the volume exponentially increasing with each successive song. In between the roof-raising choruses, the old dears let rip with slogans such as, "Praise the Lord" or, "Halleluiah!" Meanwhile, of Enid's assembled throng, the members of the St Ethel Memorial choir, feeling threatened by the singing gusto of their lay colleagues, dispatched their secret weapon. Mavis Guillegiato, of faked Italian descent, overawed the entire company with a warbling soprano to 'The Lord Is My Shepherd'.

To Enid's horror, Molly, her faithful hound, overcome by Mavis's oscillating vibrato decided to accompany the would-be opera singer with a high-pitched howling of her own. Miss Guillegiato became so incensed with the ruination of her singing efforts that she promptly kicked poor Molly harshly in the slats, whereupon the volume of Molly's ear-piercing howls doubled. Enid, seeing the suffering of her mongrel at the hands - or perhaps one should say boot - of her sister in the Lord, decided that she was no longer spiritually at one with the bitch and launched her fist in the direction of the unfortunate woman's trembling gob. Miss Guillegiato's best friend, an ex-champion female bodybuilder, who just happened to be standing in close proximity to these bizarre goings on, decided such behaviour was not acceptable without just punishment. Thereafter, revenge got the better of any Christian ideals of love and forgiveness and before long the whole room erupted into an unadulterated free for all punch-up. So from being an intended calm and peaceful rendezvous, the vigil soon escalated to a cacophony of monumental proportions. The persecuted Siberian Christians, for whom the event was intended to benefit, would probably not only have felt the spiritual ambiguity generated by their Cardiff colleagues, but would probably have heard them too.

In the adjoining terrace house next door, Rick Donovan who had been fast asleep, stirred uneasily as next door's front door bell repetitively rang and echoes of, "Welcome and Praise the Lord," filtered through his wall. But he was accustomed to sleeping in all sorts of noisy environments and initially he paid no heed to this minor infringement of his somnolence. However, whilst in the middle of a very pleasant and rather erotic dream concerning one Dr Rachel Smithers, Miss Guillegiato's rendition of 'The Lord Is My Shepherd' came booming through the long suffering adjoining wall. Rick's subconscious, on being bombarded with 'Though I walk through the valley of death' sifting through to his bedroom, seemed to take note of its master's moral decline, and Rick found himself replacing Dr Smithers' thong forthwith. Rick's sense of guilt turned precipitately into a sense of doom when Molly's wailing howls joined forces to form a duet with Miss Guillegiato, since in his dream-like state it sounded as if the hound of hell was fast approaching. Finally, when the noise of flying fists and breaking furniture pounded Rick's ears, he at last awoke with a start, thinking he probably was in hell.

Rick sat up startled by the noises filtering through the little terrace house's adjoining wall. He got up and walked down the stairs into his front hall, his senses eventually returning to him. Thereafter he faintly remembered Miss Jones's front door opening and closing and the religious nature of her houseguests' greetings to each other. "God, they're having a bloody prayer meeting next door. So what the hell is all the noise about?" Rick asked himself quizzically. Then as he realised that the old ladies must have had a disagreement with each other, he smiled to himself and listened with fascination to the verbal goings on filtering through.

"Take that you bloody bitch!" was a far cry from the initial. "Peace be with you sister." Rick picked up his stethoscope from the hall table and pressed it against the wall. He couldn't believe what was happening in his neighbours dwelling. The Gynaecologist chuckled to himself, "Enid dear, I'm so looking forward to seeing you tomorrow." But more hilarity was to come. In view of such a domestic fracas, the household across road, as well as Enid's next door neighbour on the other side had called the Police, complaining of the noise of domestic violence verging on a full scale riot.

PC Roger Jones and his partner, PC Dave Smith, had been duly dispatched and had been the first to arrive at a scene of unambiguous chaos. Both Police officers had recently failed their fitness tests on account of their portly demeanours and liking for food, as much as their dislike for exercise. They had been in the middle of a tasty takeaway and were not happy to have been interrupted. On arrival they witnessed spilling out of Enid's house, a gaggle of old ladies having a right royal go at each other. Amidst the flying fists and foul language, Miss Guillegiato lay screaming, prostrate on the front path whilst being ravaged by a little dog. The Officers called for backup and before long the entire road was amass with flashing lights and wailing sirens. Order was finally restored, but only after PC Dave Smith had sustained a black eye and his partner had suffered the indignity of a kick in the balls.

When the old dears were sufficiently subdued, they were marched or rather shuffled, pushed and helped rather unceremoniously up a step and into the back of a waiting police van for transportation to the nearest nick. It was only then that some of the Police Officers including both PC Dave Smith and PC Roger Jones had noticed their own Grannies in the throng.

"Oh my God, Gran....what the hell are you doing here?" Dave asked a little old lady with a walking stick as she hobbled past him. The old lady looked sternly at him.

"Shame on you David Smith. Shame on you for nicking your own Granny...and by the way you are much too overweight – Too many pies my boy!"

PC David Smith flushed with embarrassment, but all the Officers were now feeling distinctly uneasy about arresting a bunch of old pensioners. The final bit of good fortune for the members of the prayer group, was that the Sergeant in charge that night had witnessed his own aged mother-in-law hollering abuse and being very much part of the affray. He knew that arresting her would engender a great deal of personal suffering on his behalf at the hands of his beloved wife, and so decided against nicking any of them. Subsequently, the old dears were discharged on their way with a nothing more than a warning.

Enid in the meantime, took the Sergeant-in-charge's name and then informed him that she was good friends with the Chief of Police and would have a word, commending the proportionate and sensible actions of his Officers. Sergeant Gary Dulwit smiled pretentiously through gritted teeth and prayed that he would never have the pleasure of Enid or indeed her bloody prayer meeting ensemble, ever again. Thereafter, he watched the formidable pensioner as she called her little dog, stepped inside her little terraced house and firmly closed the front door behind her.

Rick was still chortling to himself when he climbed the stairs and got back into bed. Before snuggling down in his duvet, he checked the time and started to drift back into a deep sleep. It had just gone midnight, but before he floated back to the land of nod, he heard an ambulance's siren wailing somewhere in the distance evidently taking some poor soul into hospital.

"I hope it's not one of mine," Rick thought to himself. Little did he know.

CHAPTER 4

Paddy and Horace arrived outside Belinda's apartment to the sound of screeching brakes and the smell of burning tyre rubber. In a well-rehearsed fashion, Paddy thrust open the back doors of the ambulance, plunging the stretcher onto the concrete slabs of the pavement before racing around the side of the vehicle to join his colleague. Horace by now had picked up the medical rucksack stuffed with every imaginable emergency drug and device, and together the two paramedics burst into the apartment block and immediately set about trying to locate the whereabouts in the cursed building of Belinda's flat.

"Come on Pad, it's on the first floor, follow me." Horace smacked the lift control button and in disgust realised that the elevator was not serviceable. "Shit. Sodding thing. Looks like we'll have to burn off some of those fish and chips on the bloody stairs. Come on mate." Horace led his friend to the stairwell and together they humped the stretcher and medical kit up some rather steep concrete steps. They arrived exhausted outside number 15.

"You're sure this is it Horace?" Paddy enquired.

Horace nodded an affirmative, bent double with hands on his knees, trying to catch his breath as he did so. Paddy hammered on the door. There was no reply.

"Well I guess we'll just have to bust the bloody thing down. Did the boys in blue say they'd be attending?" Horace stammered. Paddy nodded an affirmative. "Well they are sure as hell taking their time about getting here." And with that Horace took a few steps backwards and ran like a human battering ram towards the door. His eighteen stone frame was more than enough competition for the lightweight modern door and it splintered off its hinges as Horace lunged forward landing flat on his face on the other side of the doorway. He looked up from his prostrate position on the floor and grinned. "I may be a fat bastard, but all those bloody chips have just gained us entry into this flat," Horace chuckled to himself.

The grin on his face soon evaporated when the two men searched the flat and found Belinda lying in her bedroom, barely conscious in a pool of her own blood. Her telephone was beeping and lying on the floor next to her where it had been dropped. Her dressing gown was soaked through and Belinda was white as a sheet. Horace got down on his knees beside her, felt her pulse and carried out a rapid examination as he did so.

Whilst working he whispered tenderly to her, "It's all right my lovely, there's help here now. We'll get you sorted don't you worry." As he spoke it was almost eerie how a big man with such a rough-looking exterior could be so gentle. "Pad, she's got a rapid heart rate of about 140. She's obviously bled a shedload and I reckon judging where the blood is coming from that she is either miscarrying or has a ruptured ectopic pregnancy." Horace frowned as he spoke, the concern on his face furrowing his forehead. He checked her blood pressure as Paddy struggled to get a couple of wide bore intravenous lines into her. "Blood pressure of 80/40, she's decompensating, Pad. We're gonna have to really get a move on."

The two paramedics worked proficiently and quickly. Within three to four minutes they had inserted two intravenous lines and were squeezing fluid into her to try and improve her life-threatening low blood volume. They had lifted Belinda's limp and fragile body onto the stretcher, strapping her carefully on before hurrying out of the flat towards the stairwell. Horace had injected a drug called *syntometrine* that causes contraction of the womb and so helps to reduce the bleeding from any potential miscarriage, but despite this there appeared to be no let-up in the young woman's blood loss. As they passed the broken lift Paddy swore under his breath, then together with his friend heaved the stretcher down the stairs to the waiting ambulance. Still panting from his exertions, Paddy secured the stretcher in the vehicle, whilst Horace ran back up the stairs and into the flat to fetch the medical rucksack. Paddy then jumped into the driver's seat and Horace clambered into the back of the ambulance in order to monitor Belinda's condition on the way to Accident and Emergency.

The police arrived on the scene just as the ambulance turned out of the compound. Paddy stopped the vehicle and unwound the window. "You're a bit bloody late aren't you? It is flat number 15, you need to secure it. We had to bust down the door to gain entry."

"What about you guys, do you want an escort?" asked a burly and rather red-faced copper leaning out of his window.

"No thanks boys, judging by the time it took you to get here we'd be better off being escorted by a pack of bloody snails." With that Paddy put his foot on the accelerator and the ambulance roared off down the road, leaving the red-faced copper flushed with rage. That Police Officer just happened to be PC Roger Jones, and together with his partner, PC Dave Smith, they were not having a good night shift. Both had already sustained injuries in the line of duty. One squinted through a rather blackened eye and the other hobbled as he walked with a pair of very tender goolies, courtesy of a gaggle of unruly lady pensioners at a bloody prayer meeting. To be beaten up by a bunch of old age pensioners was hardly the stuff of sorting out Cardiff's criminal underworld.

It was well after midnight by now and the roads of Cardiff lay abandoned and empty. The ambulance sped through the streets in silence, but for the reverberation of its V8 engine. Paddy had ensured that its blue light was flashing but there was no need for the siren. He picked up the handset of the radio.

"Base Papa, Base Papa, this is Fat Mama 3. We're carrying the casualty from 15 Bellview. She has sustained severe haemorrhage; I repeat - severe haemorrhage. Probable ruptured ectopic pregnancy. Please have resuscitation team awaiting our arrival with O Neg blood. Need senior gynaecologist available. Repeat - need senior gynaecologist available. Estimated arrival time seven minutes. Roger."

"Fat Mamma 3, this Base Papa, heard and understood. Out."

The radio went silent. The two paramedics concentrated on their respective jobs. Paddy drove with precision and speed, whilst his paramedic partner ensured that the IV lines kept fluid flowing into the young woman who was now his charge. Despite having 100% oxygen, the pulse oximeter attached to Belinda's finger registered falling oxygen saturations. Horace looked down in trepidation as a further trickle of blood rushed from between his patient's legs.

"Paddy mate, if your foot hasn't already floored that accelerator just friggin' do it. We really need to go like shit off a shovel if this girl's is gonna make it. Her sats are falling and she's just lost another 500 ml of the red stuff."

The ambulance was travelling at 70mph as it screeched around the final street corner and then into the hospital grounds. With the expertise of a well-practised veteran Paddy manoeuvred the vehicle so that its back doors opened out onto the entrance of the Accident and Emergency Department. Having flung open his side door he jumped down from his seat raced around to the back of the ambulance and hurled open the heavy rear doors.

"Come on Horace, let's go!" Both of them were almost short of breath with the tension. They ran with the stretcher in through the electronic doors of the Accident and Emergency department and Paddy looked around in disbelief. There was a quiet hum of gentle activity but no receiving medical crew standing by.

"Where's the frigging team to meet us? You heard me request them on the radio. Where the bloody hell are they?" Paddy shouted, the tone of his voice angry and concerned. He realised that their patient was now very sick and on the brink of haemorrhaging to death.

"Oi, you over there, this is the casualty who is bleeding to death with the probable ectopic. Now get your bloody arses busy and get us some help. Now!" Horace bellowed across the room at a group of medics and nurses who were mulling around the central station desk. They looked up in surprise at the irate paramedic and a pasty-faced young doctor, obviously only recently qualified, sauntered across to where Belinda lay unconscious. He moved irritatingly slowly and looked contemptuously at Paddy and Horace with a superior air born of inexperience.

"My name is Dr Rupert Harrington-Smythe. If you care to move aside I'll examine this patient and then a doctor will decide what is to be done." He emphasised the word 'doctor' as if Paddy and Horace were lesser mortals and as he spoke, it was with a lofty accent and an overwhelmingly supercilious manner. His colleagues shifted uncomfortably, but none contradicted him or challenged him, not even one of the experienced nurses.

Paddy and Horace looked in utter disbelief and Horace started to shake with rage. "Look you toffy-nosed little shit, we friggin' well radioed in that our patient is unconscious, bleeding to friggin' death with an estimated blood loss of two and a half litres. Her oxygen sats and blood pressure are in her boots and if we don't get her up to theatre soon, she's gonna die. Now where's the sodding gynaecologist and where's the O Neg blood we requested?"

As Horace finished his sentence the oxygen saturation monitor alarmed indicating a further decline in Belinda's wellbeing. She was now as pale as death and her breathing was rapid and shallow.

"Now look here you insolent man, I'm the doctor here and I'm in charge. And for your information, my father, Mr James Harrington-Smythe, just happens to be the chief executive of this NHS trust." Rupert Harrington-Smythe just managed to finish his sentence before Paddy smacked him a cracker in his aristocratic gob.

As Harrington-Smythe lay spread-eagled on the casualty floor, Paddy retorted, "I don't care if your daddy shits gold, I'm not going to let you kill this woman, you self-important little bastard." And with that he signalled to Horace to grab the other end of the stretcher. "Come on Horace, we'll do it ourselves," and then shouting at one of the startled nurses, "You… yes, you… phone theatres and the duty anaesthetist - tell them we are on our way up and do it now!"

The paramedics pushed the stretcher to the operating theatres and en route, Horace pulled out his mobile telephone. The tremor in his hand made it difficult to press the memory function key, but eventually he found what he was looking for. "That's it Pad, Rick Donovan, he's our man." The paramedics had got to know Rick on a mutual colleague's stag weekend and the three of them had subsequently become great friends. Horace nodded to his colleague as if trying to seek some sort of reassurance and proceeded to dial the number. "Hello, Rick. Rick, wake up man. It's Horace… yes, that's right, the paramedic. Rick, no bullshit we've just come in from a call. We've got a young woman bleeding to death. Swollen abdomen, bleeding PV, estimated two to three litres blood loss, BP and sats right down, heart rate 140. Rick I'm positive it's a ruptured ectopic pregnancy and if you don't get here quick she's had it. Please Rick... what? You're on your way. Thanks mate, see you soon... Sorry? Yes, Paddy and I are wheeling her up to theatre now. Cheers Rick, see you in a minute."

When Paddy and Horace reached the operating theatres, they were met by some worried-looking theatre staff who had fortunately just come out of the emergency theatre, having just finished off another urgent case. It took the duty anaesthetist just one look at Belinda and the readings on the monitoring equipment to realise the life and death seriousness of the situation.

The anaesthetist looked directly into Horace's eyes and calmly asked, "What do you think, boys?"

"She's bleeding PV, and has a swollen abdomen. She's lost a lot of blood. We think it's probably a ruptured ectopic," Horace replied for both the paramedics.

"Is there a surgeon on the way?"

"Yes sir, we called him as we were coming up from Casualty. It's Rick Donovan, he should be here in a few minutes."

"Thank you, gentlemen. Now please help us get her into theatre." The duty anaesthetist then addressed a member of the nursing staff. "Sister, can you please arrange for the resident gynaecologist to be bleeped. We will need whoever it is to assist Mr Donovan when he arrives."

"Certainly," she replied, and hurried to the telephone to make the necessary arrangements.

The team moved rapidly and professionally. Further intravenous access was gained, blood taken, including a full blood count, clotting studies, renal function and 6 units of blood cross-matched. In the meantime the anaesthetist had used the standby O Negative blood kept in theatre for any emergencies. Belinda was transferred to the operating table and lightly anaesthetised. In theatre no one spoke. The only noise to be heard was the rapid bleeping of the electrocardiogram in time to the patient's pulse. The anaesthetist's face looked a picture of worry; he frowned so that the skin creased on his forehead and gouged deep lines into his sweating skin. He fiddled in an agitated manner and muttered under his breath, "Come on Rick, get yourself here, we need you now." He looked down at the young woman who was his charge and whispered, "She needs you now."

CHAPTER 5

Rick replaced the telephone receiver. He delayed ploughing out of his bed by only a few seconds. As was usual when he received a telephone call in the middle of the night or the cursed bleep went off, he initially experienced a sense of being separated from reality. This was followed by transient palpitations and an uncomfortable gut-wrenching feeling that all was not well with the world, and he would be responsible for sorting out a potentially life threatening problem. Certainly he knew that if Paddy and Horace had found it necessary to telephone him well after midnight, then there had been some almighty cock-up within the hospital chain of command. Furthermore, for Horace, who was a worldly wise and experienced paramedic, to sound so worried over the phone meant that the situation was dire, to say the least. Rick threw on his clothes and ran down the stairs, picking up his car keys as he went. He sprinted out of his house and into the cold night air. As he rushed out of his front gate, he tripped on the pavement and almost went flying into Enid's old 1977 *Austin Mini,* parked carefully outside her house. It was a bizarre thought to have on his way to a medical emergency, but he rather loved that old car, and thought that even if the old biddy was an awkward customer, she had a good taste in motors.

The young gynaecologist recovered from his stumble. It was a cloudless night and a half moon greeted him as he ran along the silent empty street to reach his own car. A quick glance out of the corner of his eye and he noticed a cracked pane of glass in the front window of Miss Jones' terrace house. Rick allowed himself a wry grin as he recalled the fracas he had audibly witnessed a few hours before. He reached the corner of the road and turning into it looked in disbelief. He looked and looked again, not believing at first what his eyes were telling him. There was no sign of his beloved *Mini Cooper S*. He frantically ran up and down the length of the road just to convince himself that he hadn't parked the damn thing anywhere else. He finally stopped and stood in the empty space where he had parked his car the night before.

"Where's my bloody car gone? Oh bollocks!" Rick exclaimed aloud. "Oh God, of all the times to have your car nicked." He kicked an empty beer can in anger and disgust, the noise of it echoing down the deserted street. "Rick, now think, what to do, what to do." He knew if he ran it would take him twenty-five minutes or so to reach the hospital. He also knew that by the time he had rung for the police, ambulance service or a taxi to come and pick him up, it would probably be more than fifteen minutes for them just to arrive. Then Rick thought of Enid Jones and her *Austin Mini* parked outside her house. If he could persuade the old biddy that he needed transport to potentially save a life surely she could not refuse. Anyhow if her Christian beliefs extended to anything, now was the time that they would, in just a small way, be put the test. Rick ran back around the corner to Miss Jones's house and carefully pushed the hinged wrought-iron gate, before striding purposefully up to the front door and knocking resolutely three times.

He immediately heard Molly's blood-curdling howls and then stirrings within his neighbour's house. The light in the hall came on and the front door opened. Rick stepped back at the monstrosity standing before him. Enid was sporting a faded, worn dressing gown which she wore over the top of a high necked nightie with a white frilly collar. Her face, now devoid of makeup, was a deathly white, and her hair was misshapen and yet strangely groomed almost to perfection. Her eyes, which were sunken deep into the sockets of her skull, glared out disapprovingly at him. Molly was at her heels barking furiously at the intrusion into her mistress's privacy at such an ungodly time of the morning.

"What do you think you're playing at? Don't you know it is two o'clock in the morning? What do you want?" Miss Jones spat the words out so viciously that Rick reeled backwards at the onslaught.

Quivering, Rick summoned all his courage and then blurted out, "It's an emergency, Enid, you may not know this but I'm actually a doctor and I need to get to the hospital quickly. There's a young girl who is very unwell and I'm needed. Someone has stolen my car. Please… please can I borrow your *Mini*? It really is a matter of life and death."

"You what?" bellowed Miss Jones, whose deathly complexion had now turned crimson red with rage. "You upset me with your blasphemy and carryings on for the last year then come knocking at my door at two in the morning, waking me up in the process, to see if you can borrow my car. You impertinent young man."

"But Enid…"

"It's Miss Jones to you, you rude young hooligan."

Rick glanced down at his watch. Three precious minutes had been wasted already. Three minutes more in which the patient Rick had been informed about had time to bleed away what little blood she had. Rick looked up at Enid Jones. It didn't look as if the old girl was going to help him. It was then that he spied the set of keys hanging on a hook above a small table just inside his neighbour's hall; Rick instinctively knew those were the keys to the transport he so desperately needed. The thought of it sent his heart racing. He could feel its pounding beat almost bursting through his chest. To borrow... steal the old girl's car, it was theft. He would be banged up for it. His career would be in tatters. But what about the girl bleeding to death? 'Oh Bollocks, go for it boy,' was the last thought that went through Rick's head before he lunged forward to grab the keys.

Enid let out a spine-chilling scream as Rick made off down the short path towards the gate. "Stop thief, someone call the police. I've been robbed. Stop that thief. Help, help!" she shrieked. Her high pitched wails of torment were enough to waken every household in the street and it wasn't long before bedroom lights started to flicker on up and down the road. Meanwhile Molly had firmly attached herself with locked jaws onto Rick's left trouser leg, growling ferociously as she was dragged this way and that as Rick struggled to get away. With Molly delaying him, Rick managed to get past the gate and half way across the pavement before Enid grabbed him, jumping onto his back, her surprisingly powerful arms encircling and tightening around his exposed neck.

"Miss Jones, please you don't understand, there is a young girl who will die if I don't get to the hospital in the next few minutes, please find it in your heart to just let me borrow your car for the next hour. I promise I'll return it. Please Miss Jones… please," Rick pleaded as if his own life depended on it. His voice was hoarse and throaty since by now Enid's grip was starting to obstruct his airway. But his pleas were falling on deaf ears. Enid really had had a bad few hours. She was already mightily pissed off following the outcome of her more than lively prayer meeting. Now the little shit who was her next door neighbour was trying to nick her car. For the second time in the space of a few hours Enid found that all Christian etiquette went clean out of the window.

"You little bastard. You're no more a doctor than I'm the Queen of England, now give me my bloody keys back or I'll call the police." Then having established a firm grip on the man she considered to be a complete rogue she held on with as much ferocity as her loyal pooch, such that by now Rick was feeling the initial effects of strangulation.

For the second time in just a few hours, neighbours had started to glare out of their bedroom windows as the struggle ensued. Enid's screeching grew louder and louder, and she tightened her grasp on Rick's already obstructed windpipe so his face was now suffused with blood.

"I… I… can't breathe," Rick whispered hoarsely.

"Tough shit. Now give me back my keys." Even Enid was surprised at the deterioration in her language over the last day. Rick was too busy trying to breathe. Certainly he could have got rough and manhandled the damn woman, but did not relish the charges of assault of a defenceless old lady in addition to attempted theft. Anyway he couldn't possibly hurt the old girl, despite her blatant selfishness. It all seemed pretty hopeless and Rick was about to hand the keys back, when God intervened. Rick dropped the keys on the pavement and Enid, fast as a flash, dismounted her assailant and doubled over, bending down to pick them up. As she did so an extraordinary spectacle unfolded. Her scalp started to move across her head. Her crown of beautifully groomed hair started moving spontaneously and of its own volition, as it travelled towards the keys lying on the pavement. Rick shrieked in horror and Enid stopped dead in her tracks. The light from the moon reflected off her shiny bald scalp and, devoid of any makeup, she looked more like an Egyptian mummy than his next door neighbour. Enid immediately tried to cover her baldness with both hands before hurriedly retreating back into the inconspicuous safety of her house. She sobbed aloud as she did so, but it was too late to save hiding her secret from the majority of her neighbours, who by now were hanging from their bedroom windows, howling with laughter. As her mistress disappeared, Molly seemed to lose heart. She let go of Rick's leg and looked up at him contemptuously. Accentuated by the light from the street lamp, steam appeared to work its way up from the bottom of Rick's trousers and on his ankles he felt a warm dampness infiltrate his *Marks and Sparks* socks. Molly's parting gift before trotting back into the house was to piss on Rick. There was no doubt her bladder had been full to brimming and Enid would most certainly have approved. The keys of the Mini still lay on the pavement next to Enid's fine head of hair. Rick squelched over to where the items lay and picked them up. The neighbours, whose laughter had reached epic proportions when Molly had urinated over her foe, evidently had enjoyed watching the spectacle and were now prompting Rick to try on Enid's wig.

"Piss off the lot of you and mind your own business," Rick retorted. This only served to generate more wisecracks and jibes so Rick decided just to ignore them all. He looked at his watch; another three minutes had elapsed. He hurriedly posted Enid's wig back through her letterbox and then ran to the old girl's car. A turn of the key and the marvellous machine burst into life. Rick crunched the gear stick into first and the Mini leapt forward. Rick had lost count of the number of times he'd driven to the hospital along the same familiar stretch of road but one thing he was sure about was that it had never been so fast and it had never been in such an old car. He ignored the red traffic lights, feeling irritated that the bloody things dared to try slow him down at 2 a.m. especially since there was no bloody traffic on the road in any case. He also blatantly ignored the speed limit. In fact the Mini was probably for the first time in her aged life doubling the legal restriction.

PC Roger Jones sat slumped in the rather luxurious leather seats of the parked *BMW* Police patrol car, troughing a huge kebab. "Cheeky bastards those ambulance drivers, calling us sodding snails. I'll bloody well 'ave them." He managed to spurt the words out before cramming the next enormous portion of the succulent meat into his vacant mouth. His partner, Dave sat in the passenger seat next to him and nodded his agreement, managing a Neanderthal grunt to add to the effect. His mouth was as busy, chewing on the chips and ketchup that filled and then overflowed from it, dribbling down his chin. The policemen had so far experienced their busiest night in a while, what with violent grannies and abusive paramedics. After securing Belinda's flat and ensuring there was no hint of suspicious circumstance they had driven to the all night kebab shop to feed their voluminous stomachs. They were both well practised at devouring huge quantities of grease-dripping grub in a very short space of time, their larger than life frames being testament to the fact. In his younger days Roger had won the 'Glutton of the Year' award whilst still a trainee policeman at one of the most prestigious Police Academies in the country. It seemed only natural then to team him up with Dave (alias 'The Fat Bastard' as he was known to his friends) who during the course of a recent sabbatical in the USA, had excelled himself in American eating competitions, lifting the title 'Pig of the Month', only a short time earlier. The Cardiff criminal fraternity, who often used the derogatory term 'Pig' to describe officers of the law, had no idea that at least these two of its complement would have been proud to be called pigs. Not that Dave and Roger had ever come across many of the Cardiff criminals. It seemed rather odd that although trained to seek out and fight crime, they seemed to spend a great deal of taxpayers' money and time avoiding it. So when Rick Donovan sped past the Panda Car at 60 mph in a dilapidated Austin Mini in what was essentially a 30 mph speed limit they initially paid it little attention.

"Oh let it go Rog. After all I haven't even finished my second portion of chips yet."

"Yeah, you're right Dave. Why ruin a perfectly good meal?" his partner replied.

It was then that there was a crackle over the radio and the operator's voice clearly informed them of a stolen 1977 *Austin Mini* heading in their general direction for the local hospital. As if to reinforce the message, the sergeant on duty grabbed the microphone and now let his feelings be known to the pair of them. "If you're both sitting there filling your fat faces instead of catching crooks - which is what I suspect you're doing - then listen up. That stolen Mini belongs to Miss Enid Jones, a close friend of the

Chief Inspector, and I believe it is the same old lady we had dealings with earlier in the evening." Sergeant Gary Dulwit took a breath then continued, "After tonight's escapade, I have no desire to cross that ferocious pensioner again, I am not paid enough!" Sergeant Dulwit shuddered at the thought of being once again on the receiving end of Enid's fiery temper, "So gentlemen you'd bloody well better catch the sod you has nicked her car or we are all for the high jump. Do you hear me?"

Dave and Roger looked at the radio rather sheepishly, not knowing quite how to respond.

"Do you bloody hear me?" The sergeant's tone was becoming distinctly hostile.

Roger reluctantly put down the remnants of his kebab, shoved the unfinished food under his seat and simultaneously started up the BMW's impressive engine, grabbing the handset of the radio as he did so. "Affirmative, Sarge. Err… we've just seen the suspect speeding past and are in hot pursuit. Out."

The powerful patrol car swept out from the layby and started after the *Mini,* siren sounding and flashing lights blazing.

"Nothing wrong with getting into the Sergeant's good books, not to mention the Chief's now, is there

Davey-boy? And this one shouldn't be too strenuous."

"Too right. Let's get the bastard," Dave subtly replied.

Rick Donovan was driving the ancient vehicle to almost the limit of its capability when he heard the distant warble of a siren becoming stronger by the minute. The flashing lights in his rear view mirror confirmed his worst fears. "Oh sodding hell, not now. Please, not bloody well now," Rick groaned to himself. He knew the hospital was only another quarter of a mile up the road, he was almost there. Visions of a young woman haemorrhaging to death crossed his mind as he pushed his right foot the last half an inch on the accelerator pedal so that it was now flat on the floor. The *Mini* responded beautifully to the task, and with engine howling, steering wheel shaking and the whole frame of the little car vibrating violently her speedometer needle touched 75 mph.

"Frigging 'ell! The bastard is trying to outrun us!" Roger exclaimed in utter disbelief. "He must be stark raving bonkers if he reckons he's gonna get away in that heap of crap."

The *BMW* started to close and Rick knew that it would be a close shave. He willed the old machine to just get to the hospital gates before the police caught them. He would then have at least half a chance to escape from them for the time being. "Come on old girl, come on. Nearly there." Rick patted the Mini's dashboard encouragingly as the little car reached the hospital gates with the Police now only yards behind. The Mini screeched to a halt outside the main entrance to the hospital, and leaving the car door flung open, Rick ran through the electronic doors and into the maze of corridors that led up to the main operating theatre. Roger and David were left trailing a long way behind. They were both out of breath after running to the hospital entrance, their copious quantities of blubber slowing them down sufficiently for Rick to escape.

The gynaecologist checked his watch. It had taken him five minutes to reach the hospital, plus more precious minutes grappling with Enid, but the little *Mini* had proudly done its job. "So far so good, now let's get this young woman sorted out," he thought to himself. Having rapidly changed, he donned a mask, a theatre hat and scrubbed up, then slipped through the door into Theatre Eight. The atmosphere was thick with tension and the seriousness of their patient's predicament was evident on the strained faces of his colleagues. Rick just hoped that he wasn't too late.

CHAPTER 6

It was 2:15 am. While Rick had been enduring near strangulation courtesy of his aged neighbour, and then a death defying car chase in an ancient Mini as he tried to reach his hospital, the duty Senior House Officer, Dr Rachel Smithers had run in her operating blues half way across the hospital to the main operating theatre complex. Her bleep had gone off a number of times and she had rushed to where Belinda Jones lay bleeding to death. Then just before her arrival, her fast bleep had let out the chilling "Cardiac Arrest! Cardiac Arrest! Dr Rachel Smithers to the main operating theatres immediately."

Rachel had literally sprinted the last bit of distance, down the stairwell and along the main corridors to the operating suites. When she arrived she was out of breath and her heart was pounding. The sight that greeted her on arrival in operating Theatre Eight filled her with dread. The patient had been intubated and ventilated and members of the arrest team were taking it in turns to administer cardiac massage. Blood was running into the patient via two wide-bore intravenous lines in her arms and a central line pierced the delicate skin of her neck and ran on into her carotid vein. The skin of her face and chest was so very pale - deathly pallor, they called it - and she looked so young, so vulnerable and so very beautiful. Amidst the lines and the wires and the monitoring equipment there lay a person precariously perched on the dividing line between life and death. Rachel identified with her immediately for they were contemporaries, both roughly the same age. The young Senior House Officer shivered with fear, and anxiety mixed with inadequacy permeated her being. Was she now to be responsible for opening this young woman's belly? What if she couldn't stop the bleeding, would she be responsible for her death? That having been said, Rachel knew if the young woman didn't survive her cardiac arrest there would be no surgery anyway. She held her breath as the anaesthetic team worked.

The anaesthetist gave a stern order. "Stand back, everyone clear." He had applied the electrodes to Belinda's naked chest and now Rachel stood mesmerised as the body of this young woman violently jolted upwards as the electric current shot through her youthful frame. The team looked up apprehensively at the cardiac monitor and quiet prayers went around the room. Everyone held their breath.

"Oh thank God, she's back with us." The anaesthetist broke the silence and the relief was palpable. "Someone get me some more blood - and where the hell is the surgeon?"

Rachel edged forwards although almost reluctantly. She scrubbed then hurriedly cleaned and draped the patient before her, trying to give the impression of an easy confidence. But inside she was feeling anything but assured. Her hand shook as she applied the knife to the skin of Belinda's soft white belly and made her first incision. The scalpel went through the skin and subcutaneous fat like a knife through butter. Then she went down through muscle, through the sheath and on into the peritoneal cavity. Coils of small and large intestine bulged out of the incision and squirmed over the freshly draped green surgical towels. Blood brimmed up to and then over the edge of the wound, litres of it that had bled from her ruptured ectopic pregnancy. Then Rachel felt fear. A fear of inadequacy, of responsibility, of being unable to cope. It ravaged and tore away at her confidence; a fear that every novice surgeon experiences when faced with a critical and life threatening situation. Rachel's face was almost as pale as the exsanguinated patient before her. Sweat dripped from her forehead and her heart raced with terror. She wanted to run, to escape if only to avoid the task in front of her.

"Blood pressure is dropping again. We're not keeping up with fluid replacement. Rachel, you're going to have to clamp that bleeder off pretty quickly or else we are going to lose her! Rachel, do you hear me?" The anaesthetist looked at her kindly and spoke gently. He knew that her inexperience hampered her and was afraid now that the situation was beyond her. Dr Rachel Smithers felt herself becoming faint and started to sway on her feet. Panic was starting to take hold, and then from behind her, there was a God sent, quiet whisper, a voice she was never more relieved to hear.

"Rachel, do you want me to take over?" The sound of Rick's voice immediately lifted a huge burden from her young shoulders and the weight of responsibility for this woman's life was swiftly taken from her. Rachel was never more relieved.

"Oh Rick, am I glad to see you. I can't find the bleeding vessel, the pelvis just keeps refilling with blood so that it's almost impossible to see anything and I can't…"

Rick stopped her in mid-flow. "Thank you for preparing and opening the pelvis for me, perhaps I'll finish off." He spoke so calmly and with such benevolence towards her that her failing confidence returned. Addressing the operating Theatre Sister, Rick quietly asked, "Suction please Sister, and a steady stream of large swabs."

The Theatre Sister passed the suction catheter and Rachel started to hoover up litres of the young woman's blood. This cleared Rick's field of view and the gynaecologist plunged his gloved hand deep into Belinda's bleeding abdomen. He worked for a number of seconds, his only sense that of touch being guided by his sound knowledge of pelvic anatomy. Blood continued to pour from the wound and the anaesthetist looked on anxiously as another one of his monitors alarmed.

"Rick, you know she has arrested already. I don't think she can take much more of this."

Rick Donovan ignored the comment. He already knew the gravity of the situation. He doggedly persevered, although his theatre blues were drenched in his own sweat and he could feel and almost hear the palpitations of his heart pounding in his head, he persevered. Then Rachel noticed it first; a change of expression on his face, a slow blink, the relaxation of his taut shoulders, a look of relief and then almost a smile.

"Large curved clamp please, Sister." Rick lifted from the pool of blood, deep in the young woman's abdomen, a ruptured ectopic pregnancy. There was a rhythmic arterial spurt of blood from the centre of it. Rick quickly clamped the offending lesion and the bleeding instantly stopped. "Got it, the bastard." Rick uttered the simple statement and the relief in that operating theatre was almost palpable. Everyone relaxed and the stony silence was broken. As blood continued to be poured in through the wide-bore drips, the young woman's blood pressure and pulse started to stabilise. Rick stole a quick look at the anaesthetist who had been instrumental in keeping this young woman alive prior to his arrival. There was a mutual nod of respect and thanks before Rick set about finishing off his operation. He excised the ectopic pregnancy before suturing off the remaining blood vessel pedicles. The residual blood was washed out of the patient's abdomen and her fallopian tube and ovary on the other side were checked. When Rick was confident that there was no other source of bleeding, he placed a drain in the pelvic cavity and sutured the layers of tissue to close the young woman's abdomen.

As the last stitch was tied, Rick looked up at Rachel and smiled. "That was bloody difficult. I don't know about you but I could feel my old heart racing! That bleeding ectopic was deep in the pelvis and those loops of bowel certainly didn't help. Anyhow, job done eh?" Rachel nodded, before Rick continued, "Rachel, I think she should probably go to the Intensive Care Unit, certainly for the first twenty-four hours. She's just about lost her own volume in blood and she will need close monitoring and fluid replacement. Can you arrange it for me?"

"No worries boss. Oh, and Rick… thank you." Rachel looked him straight in the eye her sincerity was evident for all to see. They disrobed from their blood stained theatre gowns and washed. In the heat of the moment Rick had almost forgotten the events that preceded his arrival at the hospital. After thanking the theatre staff, he and Rachel strolled out of the double doors of the main operating theatres, chatting and laughing.

"Do we still have a date for Friday night then Mr Donovan?" As Rachel asked the question, two rather obese police officers came forward out of the shadows of the corridor.

"I am afraid, Missy, that Dr Donovan here ain't going to be able to take anyone out for dinner for a little while." Then, turning to Rick, the larger of the two policemen stuttered, "Richard Donovan, I am arresting you for the theft of a motor vehicle belonging to Miss Enid Jones. You have the right to remain silent. Anything you say may be used in evidence…" Roger spelt out the required formal jargon of the arrest surprisingly well, considering he had not arrested anyone for a very long time.

Dr Rachel Smithers flipped. "What the hell is going on? Rick, who are these two jokers?"

Rick hung his head. "Oh God, Rachel, I had to borrow – well, maybe take - my next door neighbour's car. Mine got stolen. It was the only way to get to the hospital in time." There was a moment's silence before Rick looked up. "And you know what, if it meant saving that young woman's life I'd bloody well do it again."

Rachel turned to the two coppers with her most venomous of looks. "You're surely not going to arrest Mr Donovan? He has just saved a young woman's life. If he hadn't taken that car and arrived here in the nick of time we'd have had a bloody funeral on our hands. Do you hear me? He did it to save her life.

You can't arrest him. He's a flipping hero not a common criminal." As if to reinforce what Rachel had been saying, two porters accompanied by a theatre nurse wheeled Belinda Jones out from the double doors and across to the Intensive Care Unit. The array of tubes, beeping monitors and wires attached to the young woman were testament to the severity of her condition.

The team stopped briefly when they reached Rick. "Mr Donovan sir, Horace and Paddy send their kindest regards and thanks. They had to rush off, apparently another call."

Rick smiled at the passing team. "Please give them my best and thank them for me." By now the two policemen were looking distinctly uncomfortable. It was more than obvious that Rick's motive for stealing Enid's battered old banger was entirely honourable to say the least. In different circumstances they might even have tried to circumvent arresting him had it not been for the stern words their sergeant had echoed on the radio on the road up to the hospital.

"I am very sorry sir, but theft is theft no matter how honourable your intentions. I am afraid you are under arrest and will have to accompany us down to the station." As he spoke, PC Roger Jones placed handcuffs on the gynaecologist's wrists. Rachel Smithers was almost in tears as she reached up and kissed Rick before he was led away by the two burly coppers. As it happened PCs Roger Smith and David Jones had absolutely no sense of direction and after 10 minutes of walking they had led Rick to no further than the hospital canteen.

"How sweet of you… you've brought me here for a cup of coffee and a muffin before my incarceration?" Rick joked.

The two coppers were warming to their captive and to Rick's surprise agreed to the late night snack on condition that Rick show them the way out thereafter. It was some time before they all finally arrived at the Police station. Dave and Roger had more than a muffin each.

Despite the discomfort of the cast iron bunk Rick had never slept better. The cold, bare walls of the police cell did not signify a prison keeping him in, so much as a fortress keeping others out. Furthermore, joy of joys, his bleep could go off as many bloody times as it liked, it did not matter. He was now exempt from any responsibility regarding any patients since the police force (what a marvellous institution,

Rick concluded) had made it impossible for him to carry out any doctors' duties. The police constable who showed him to his cell had been astonished to find Rick so grateful for the meagre accommodation on offer. In truth it was no worse than many of the on-call rooms Rick had frequented throughout his junior doctor years. More importantly, he had fallen asleep with a clear conscience in the knowledge that the life of a human being had been saved that day. As Mr Donovan closed his eyes, he thought about the events of the preceding evening. The phone call, his stolen car, the acquisition of his next door neighbour's Mini, the police chase and finally the dramatic events in the operating theatre. His mind focused in on the young woman whose life he had saved. He saw her face, young and so beautiful. God, she really was beautiful. His mind slowly drifted into blissful somnolence and he smiled inwardly. "Thank you Enid. Sorry about the wig."

CHAPTER 7

The Duty Officer opened the small viewing shutter on the heavy steel door of the cell and peeped in. Rick Donovan was still fast asleep. The breakfast that had been brought to him at 7 a.m. lay untouched on the small table adjacent to the bunk.

"Poor bugger, he must be knackered to sleep like a baby on that bed," the copper mused as he quietly closed the shutter to let Rick continue his slumber. The news of the surgeon's imprisonment had obviously spread. The police station had received innumerable telephone calls from various quarters asking why Rick was being held in a cell like some common criminal, since if anything he was a hero. While most of the callers had been reasonably civil in their questioning and messages, a few had been damn right hostile. A paramedic called Horace had telephoned to demand Dr Donovan's immediate release or else he would personally see to it that the police had their backsides sued off. Dr Rachel Smithers was apparently organising a junior doctors' revolt and a demonstration on her colleague's behalf. The Cardiff Chief of Police had been contacted by a local journalist and asked for his comments on the arrest and imprisonment of a doctor who had gone beyond the call of duty to save his patient's life. All in all it appeared that Rick's arrest had caused quite a stir, at least locally.

While all this was going on, Rick slept on oblivious, his mind embroiled in a dreamy sleep. In his reverie, he revelled in dreams of being surrounded by scantily clad blondes on a beach in Barbados. One of the blondes who had a particularly nice smile was holding a chilled glass of Chablis to his lips, whilst another held a colourful sunshade over him to protect him from the baking sun. All the while he bathed his feet in the gentle clear water of the Caribbean. One of the stunning women reached down to touch his arm. Even in his dream Rick felt her hand to be uncannily real. He reached up to tenderly pull her down towards him in order to kiss her, when from out of nowhere he heard, "Get off me you bastard!"

Rick was roused from his erotic slumber with some haste. He found the hand that he had grasped was not delicate, slim and silky, but large, callused and hairy. He opened his eyes to see Sergeant Dulwit leaning over him, and obviously struggling to get away. Rick let the policeman's hand go and Dulwit flew backwards at a rate of knots, landing with a thump on the concrete cell floor.

"Bloody gynaecologists! My mother warned me about people like you! What the hell do you think you were doing?"

"Sergeant, I do apologise. I was having a dream you see…"

"I honestly do not wish to know the contents of your erotic escapades, whether you are fully awake or indeed when you are asleep," Dulwit grumbled as he climbed up off the floor and brushed himself down.

"I can only apologise Sergeant."

"All right, Dr Donovan I accept your apology. No harm done eh?"

"Sure," Rick replied. "Anyhow, what are you doing in my cell and why did you wake me up? Honestly, I haven't had such a good sleep in ages."

"Umm…I hear that you Medics do work quite hard", Dulwit had got over having his hand grabbed and was warming to his prisoner once again.

Rick took advantage and looking pleadingly at the

Police Sergeant asked, "Are you going to release me and has Enid relented? Or am I to be banged up for a bit longer?"

"I'm afraid we can't release you just yet. Your bail and the associated paperwork will take a wee while to sort out," Dulwit responded.

"In which case can I just be left in peace to sleep please?" Rick was slightly annoyed at the intrusion into his rather tantalising dream life.

"Oh....yes...sorry, Doctor." But the good Sergeant didn't take the hint and remained standing motionless in Rick's cell. Then weirdly he started to fidget nervously and looked most uncomfortable. "Dr Donovan... since I am here now, I wonder if you'd mind... um... am I right in thinking you are a gynaecologist?"

"Well, I assume that since your outburst pertaining to the fact that all gynaecologists were perverts was directed at me, you had sort of figured that out."

"Oh, err, sorry, Doc. It's just that I wondered if I might ask your advice." Dulwit hesitated sheepishly.

Rick remained silent but looked directly at Dulwit, raising his eyebrows and looking surprised for effect. The good Sergeant Dulwit managed to find some courage from somewhere and blurted out, "It's about a personal matter you see."

Rick sighed. He was getting used to carrying out impromptu consultations in some of the weirdest places, but he had to admit he had never experienced giving advice whilst being banged up in a police cell. However, having thought about the request, it certainly wouldn't do any harm to make friends with a copper, especially considering his predicament. "My dear Sergeant, please ask away."

"Well, it's the wife, Doc." There followed a rather prolonged pause.

"Yes. What about your wife?" Rick encouraged.

"Well, she doesn't seem to be as, how can I put it, as amorous as before." Sergeant Dulwit was by now the colour of beetroot.

"Before what?" Rick asked matter-of-factly.

"Well, you know, before her periods all stopped." Dulwit could feel himself blushing.

Rick looked Sergeant Dulwit up and down. He decided that the grey, balding hair and lines on his face, together with his general demeanour, must have made him about fifty years old. If his beloved wife were roughly the same age, she would no doubt be menopausal. "How old is your wife, Sergeant?"

"She's fifty-one."

"And do you happen to know when exactly her last period was?"

"Oh, well over a year ago, I guess." The police officer was becoming less embarrassed as time went on.

"So that makes her menopausal all right. Does she suffer with night sweats, hot flushes, poor sleep, or even problems with being a bit dry down below when you have intercourse?"

"Now you come to mention it she does complain of sweating and flushes and when we have a bit of … you know, hanky panky, it's a bit like sticking the old boy into a love tunnel of sandpaper, although I would never tell my beloved that!" Sergeant Dulwit walked morosely over to the police cell bunk and sat down beside the gynaecologist.

"And I take it that Mrs Dulwit isn't taking HRT?" Rick enquired.

"No, I don't think so." Dulwit looked up hopefully.

Then quite extraordinarily, the young gynaecologist explained in some detail to his captor how Hormone Replacement Therapy worked and that Mrs Dulwit sounded as if she needed it to get her life back together. Rick further reassured the good police officer that it would also soften and moisten his wife's 'love tunnel', as Sergeant Dulwit called it, and therefore might well help with her ailing libido. Rick further explained that if problems with libido persisted despite HRT, another treatment in the form of a 'testosterone' implant was likely to improve matters.

As he explained the pros and cons of HRT to the attentive Sergeant Dulwit and in particular the benefits to be had with regard to a decent love life, he had a flashback to a past patient who he had seen in Sir John Rawarse's clinic. She had complained of poor libido despite already being on HRT. The patient had readily agreed to have a testosterone implant inserted, which Rick had duly done before organizing to see her in clinic six weeks later. The six weeks had soon rolled around and Rick remembered her returning to clinic. He had been in the middle of a consultation with another patient who was enthusiastically complaining about a number of her various gynaecological ailments when all sorts of strange groaning noises filtered through the thin stud wall from the adjoining consulting room.

Eyebrows had been raised and his patient tittered, "Blimey Doc, you sure this is just a medical establishment?"

Ignoring the comment, Rick had excused himself, got up from behind his desk and sauntered out to the nurses' station. The moaning and panting that had emanated from Sir John's consulting room could be clearly heard even in the waiting area. Patients were fidgeting nervously as the gasps and verbal expressions of ecstasy reached a crescendo and then waned to stony silence once again. Rick had asked the clinic Sister what the hell was going on as the moans had started up again.

"Streuth! It's bloody well starting again. Sis, what the hell is going on?" The clinic sister had whispered that it was the same patient that Rick had given a testosterone implant to six weeks earlier. The GP had written a desperate letter stating that the woman's poor husband was exhausted and it was his opinion that the wretched woman had developed 'Spontaneous Orgasm Syndrome'. After the third orgasm had been heard reverberating around the gynaecology clinic, Sir John Rawarse, face red with undisguised embarrassment and horror, had hurried to the sanctuary of the nurse's station. His mortification had been doubled by the strange and enquiring looks of the patients in the waiting room when they had witnessed him hastily emerge. Rick had quickly returned to his own consulting room to let the old man get on with it.

"Doc, Doc, you alright?" Sergeant Dulwit enquired bringing Rick back to the present and his current incarceration in a police cell.

"Oh, sorry Sergeant, was just reminiscing." Rick shook his head. He chuckled to himself. "No wonder Rawarse ended up having a coronary, poor bastard."

The impromptu consultation appeared to go down well and Sergeant Dulwit appeared to be most grateful for Rick's advice, although he admitted he wasn't too keen on testosterone implants for his beloved wife. Visions of a bearded beloved with a deep voice made the copper shudder, although he seemed very keen on the standard HRT. "I'll make an appointment with the GP, and drag my wife along. Dr Donovan, thank you so much for listening to me and for your advice." The police officer stood up and grabbing Rick's hand shook it with gusto. "I am sorry that I shouted at you when I first came in, silly misunderstanding I suppose. I'll hurry up the paperwork for your release, and we'll see if we can't get you out of here as quickly as possible. Please bear with us Dr Donovan." With that he left Rick to return to his slumbers.

Rick awoke again with a start. He had slept for a

further six uninterrupted, solid hours. He recalled his spontaneous consultation with Dulwit and thoughts of testosterone implants made him smile. 'I wish I had Spontaneous Orgasm Syndrome,' he thought to himself. Considering he was banged up at the local police station he found himself in remarkably good spirits, but it was partly because he was now less sleep deprived.

There was a clunk from the heavy steel door as the lock was turned and a fresh faced young policewoman entered. "Good afternoon Dr Donovan, I trust you slept well. I've brought you a late lunch."

"Well that's very kind, thank you. Now officer, I wonder could you please tell me what is going on with regard to my incarceration in this establishment. Despite your wonderful hospitality I really am quite anxious to be a free man again." Rick really did feel a great deal better after his slumber.

The young policewoman looked surprisingly shy; she was evidently reasonably new to the game. She leant over to where Rick was sitting, "Well sir, we are all anxious to release you and drop all charges in view of the mitigating circumstances", and then dropping her voice to a quiet conspiratorial tone, "We all think that you are a hero after what you did. Oh and by the way, my name is Sally." The young woman flushed as she spoke and she was definitely not menopausal.

It was Rick's turn to blush, "Golly, thank you so much um… Sally."

The young policewoman continued, "But Dr Donovan I am afraid that Miss Jones would appear to be adamant that you face criminal charges. In fact I believe she is coming in later to make a statement."

"I see. Sounds serious. The old bat has obviously got it in for me."

"It would appear so, sir. But I do have some good news for you."

"Really, apart from a criminal record, loss of my job and the likely discontinuation of my registration with the General Medical Council…" Rick snapped tersely and then regretted saying this almost as soon as he had spoken it. He stopped himself as the young police woman looked bereft. "I do apologise, you have been nothing but kind and I am just feeling sorry for myself. Forgive me, you have some good news for me?" Rick gently smiled at the young woman in front of him.

Police Constable Sally Johnston moved closer to Rick, "Your bail was paid this morning and Sergeant Dulwit has completed the paperwork. You are free to leave, but I do have to ask you to stay in Cardiff until a court hearing is arranged."

Rick looked at Sally Johnston quizzically, "Oh right. Yes that is good news. Incidentally, you don't happen to know who paid the bail do you?"

"The paperwork states a gentleman by the name of Sir John Rawarse, I believe," Sally replied.

"Bloody hell, his cardiac arrest must have affected his brain!" then looking up at the Policewoman in front of him, "Sorry, it is just that I was not expecting it to be him and thank you, yes that is good news." Rick laughed out loud and was secretly quite chuffed that the old man had acted supportively. It boded well for the inevitable hospital investigation and witch-hunt that was bound to occur in the near future. Rick graciously declined the late lunch, again thanked PC Sally Johnston, signed for and collected his few belongings and made his way home, courtesy of the number 9 bus.

CHAPTER 8

It was a miserable morning. The rain pelted down in bursts only to be replaced by a murky drizzle that whirled around on gusts of wind that rattled the front window of the old terrace house. Enid, although feeling thoroughly miserable with herself, started her daily chores. Her faithful hound, Molly, sat in her usual place on the hearthrug as her mistress carried out her work. But even Molly looked melancholic this morning. Enid dusted around her collection of ornaments on the mantelpiece, humming, 'O come abide with me' as she cleaned. The trauma of the previous evening meant that she had not managed to sleep a wink. Her wig, which had been washed and groomed to perfection, sat conspicuously on the top of the banister at the bottom of the stairs. She thought of the fiasco of the doomed prayer meeting and how her position within her local church would now most certainly be compromised. She thought of the neighbours having a sly giggle at her expense following the rather embarrassing revelations of her bald pate the night before. Yet Enid Jones was not one to be unduly influenced by idle gossip and was sufficiently thick-skinned to carry on with life no matter what. Yet she was also determined that the thug who had so cruelly exposed her rather bad baldness should meet a suitably harsh fate. The telephone rang.

"Hello?"

"Oh hello, could I speak to a Mrs Enid Jones please."

"It's Miss Jones here whoever you are, who is this?" Enid asked sharply.

"Oh, I beg your pardon, madam, this is Sergeant Dulwit from your local police station… you may remember we u-m-m-m…met, and u-m-m-m later spoke on the telephone last night." There was stony silence from Enid. "You'll be pleased to know we've recovered your car and I am pleased to say it is absolutely fine…no damage at all. Oh and we caught the man who took it. Your next door neighbour, a Mr Donovan I believe."

"I am glad to hear you've caught the scoundrel, Sergeant. Now how long is he going to be in jail?"

"Um… well Mrs… errr… Miss Jones…" Sergeant Dulwit nervously hesitated. "I'm afraid we are probably going to let him go later today."

"You what?" shrieked Enid in the most shrill and piercing voice.

"Well ma'am, you see we kept him overnight in a cell until further questioning had taken place, but it would appear this morning there were extenuating circumstances that are in Mr Donovan's favour."

Sergeant Dulwit's explanation tailed off into a mere whisper as he heard the grinding of Enid's false teeth through the earpiece of the telephone. Back in her terrace house, duster in hand, Enid started to shake with fury. Her bald head and face filled with the blood red of rage. "You bloody bastards!" she screamed down the telephone with all the frustration her battered bald ego could muster. Sergeant Dulwit, who was used to such comments issuing forth from the pierced lips of punks, skinheads, football hooligans and other such foulmouthed low life, really didn't expect it from a seventy plus year old, church-going granny with a pooch called Molly.

"Well really, madam, I really don't think there is any need for that," he exclaimed in a voice of genuine surprise.

"I don't give a monkey's backside what you think you ignorant little man." There was a gulp of amazement on the other end of the phone and even Enid surprised herself with the further obscenities coming from her mouth, and to a police officer of all people. Yet the thought of Rick Donovan not paying a heavy price for the humiliation reaped upon her, filled Enid with a kind of moral outrage. Yet still she managed to calm herself. 'Be civil, calm down, calm down,' the pensioner thought to herself.

Sergeant Dulwit tactfully ignored the last comment regarding his physical and intellectual stature. "Perhaps, Miss Jones, if you understood the extenuating circumstances surrounding Mr Donovan's behaviour, it might…" The Sergeant was cut short by the ferocious onslaught of Enid's slightly more controlled outburst.

"Now look here Officer Dulwit, that man…" Enid shuddered just thinking about him. "That man lied about some ridiculous story of him being a doctor, attacked me, humiliated me in front of all my neighbours and then stole my car. Now you lovey-dovey fairy boys are telling me that the bastard's had a hard life and there are extenuating circumstances. Is that right, Officer Dulwit? The innocent and the helpless suffer again because the namby-pamby boys in blue have turned into a bunch of left wing woofters."

Sergeant Dulwit had some difficulty imagining Enid to be either innocent or helpless, and was becoming increasingly irked by her derogatory comments. He became slightly firmer in his manner. "Miss Jones, he wasn't lying to you. Rick Donovan is a doctor. He is a gynaecologist. On the night in question he was on call…"

"Lies, more lies," Enid again cut him short.

"It most certainly is not a lie, Miss Jones." Dulwit's tone became more authoritative. He continued. "Last night Mr Donovan saved the life of a young woman who would most definitely have died if he had been unable to get to the hospital. If he had not acted as he did that young woman would be lying in the mortuary as we speak. Now if you so wish you can press charges and make things difficult for Mr Donovan. That of course is up to you."

"What about my friend, the Chief Inspector, what does he think?" Enid purposefully exaggerated 'my friend' to ensure that Dulwit was once again aware she had connections in high places.

Sergeant Dulwit smiled to himself. "The Chief, who I can assure you has been kept up to date with all the relevant facts on the case, wants any charges against Dr Donovan dropped on account of the mitigating circumstances."

For a few seconds there was a silent truce. Enid thought back to the events of the previous night. The scumbag had said he was a doctor and that he urgently needed to get to the hospital because of some very sick patient. A matter of 'life and death' he had said. Perhaps in calmer moments Enid would have relented and seen sense. Yet the old-age pensioner was so incensed by the humiliation suffered at the hands of her neighbour that she had blocked any rational thought out. Her pride got the better of her and all she wanted was retribution.

"I don't care what the Chief says. That man unlawfully took my car without my permission after forcibly grabbing my keys. I want him charged, do you hear me, Dulwit?"

Sergeant Dulwit sighed. "Yes Miss Jones, if that is your wish I'll send a car to come and pick you up later this afternoon. We'll complete your statement and finish off any other paperwork then."

"Good. Thank you, Sergeant. I shall mention you to the Chief." Enid spoke condescendingly, rather like an old school mistress addressing one of her pupils.

"Don't bother, you old bag," Dulwit whispered as he put down the phone.

Enid finished her household chores, called the window company to organise a new pane of glass for the cracked front window and ensured there was no sign of any debris from the unfortunate happenings of the night before. It was late afternoon when the panda car arrived outside the old terrace house. Enid had donned her wig, best coat and scarf and was ready and waiting when the two police officers knocked at her front door.

PCs Roger Jones and David Smith were back at work. They both moaned when their Sergeant gave them their orders to pick up Enid and bring her to the station to make a statement. It really was the very last thing on earth that either of them wanted to do. That having been said they both acted professionally and with the utmost courtesy, despite having been assaulted by the members of Enid's prayer meeting, less than 24 hours beforehand. However, they both silently objected to having to transport Enid's Mutt, especially when she pulled out a half finished kebab from under Roger's front seat.

Enid reacted instantly. "This is a disgrace! Smelly, half-chewed bits of meat lying around rotting in a police car. You should both be ashamed. Do you hear me?"

"Err… yes Miss Jones." Roger remembered shoving the unfinished takeaway under his seat just before giving chase to his passenger's stolen car the night before. Under Enid's glare he felt like a chastised schoolboy, not an adult officer of the law. Molly gratefully finished off the unexpected meal, after which she showed her appreciation by passing the most malodorous wind imaginable. The odour was repugnant to say the least and filled the entire car. Enid kept absolutely still, eyes straight ahead. Roger and Dave shifted uncomfortably in their seats, and Roger opened the electric window to give a little light relief to his nostrils.

When they finally arrived at the police station, Enid took Molly up into her arms, got out of the car, then turning to Roger she remarked, "As for you, young man, may I suggest you see a doctor. Your bowels are obviously rotten to the core." With that the cantankerous old woman marched with her little dog through the main doors of the police station and up to the reception desk.

Sergeant Dulwit greeted her with forced politeness. "Good afternoon Miss Jones, this way please."

He led the old woman and her dog into one of the interrogation rooms to take a full written and signed statement. There was a young female Police Officer waiting to complete the paper work with her Sergeant. She stood up and smiled at Enid when the old lady entered the room and Enid immediately warmed to her. Molly allowed herself to be stroked by the young woman and even affectionately nuzzled up against her.

"You remind me of my beloved niece young lady. She is kind, sensible and lovely just like you, which is so refreshing after having to deal with your other colleagues", and with that Enid stole a malevolent glare at Sergeant Dulwit, who visibly grimaced.

"Oh thank you Miss Jones, that is very kind of you to say so." The young woman's beaming smile was cut short after an irritated Dulwit elbowed her.

After an hour or so the necessary paperwork had been completed. Sergeant Dulwit tentatively asked her once more, "Miss Jones, are you absolutely sure that you want to proceed with the pressing of all charges, despite knowing that Dr Donovan took your car for the express purpose of getting to the hospital to save a young woman's life and I have to say a young woman much the same age as Police Officer Sally here?" Dulwit's eyes settled on his female colleague.

But Enid was unrelenting and was irritated. "Do you think I would have dragged myself out in this appalling weather, or braved a kebab-ridden panda car and a police officer with a flatulence problem to sit here for an hour listening to you prattle on with your questions if I didn't want to press charges? No offence to you young lady."

Dulwit sighed. "I take it that means you want to press ahead, madam?"

"Yes, Officer, that is correct. I want that man to pay for what he did to me."

Later that evening, a driver employed by the Police returned Enid's 1977 *Austin Mini* and parked the trusty classic on the road outside her little terraced house.. The delivery driver knocked on Enid's front door and got her to sign for a white envelope with the Mini's key inside together with paperwork confirming that the little car had been thoroughly checked over. The insurance company had been informed and had subsequently accepted, that although Enid's car had been taken without her consent, there was absolutely no evidence of any malicious or any other damage. In fact her *Mini* had been given a good clean and topped up with petrol. The old lady was delighted to have her old motor back, sitting outside her house, but remained obstinately unrepentant and unbelieving, when it came to the young man who was her next door neighbour.

CHAPTER 9

Rick had hoped for a lift home, and in fact PC Sally Johnston had volunteered to drive him, but her request was denied and following Rick's release, he was directed to the local bus stop. Predictably the number 9 bus was 20 minutes late, the bus shelter was non-existent and Rick got utterly soaked as the heavens opened and pissed on him with exaggerated disdain. As the number 9 bus pitched up, so too did the number 10, number 11, and number 13. "Sodding buses!" Rick muttered as he boarded the public transport. An hour later he was home. He jumped lightly off the bus and made his way down the cobbled street lined with identical terraced houses. As he reached his front gate, the upstairs window of the house across the road opened and a middle-aged, rather burly looking man hung out of it.

"Good on yer, Rick. That old cow has had it coming for a long time now. Didn't know she was bald as a coot though." He laughed mockingly at Miss Jones's misfortune.

Rick ignored the obnoxious neighbour and was glad he did so when he saw Enid peering through her net curtains. She quickly turned and looked away and he felt a pang of sorrow for her. She really was a mixed-up, bitter old bat and despite the obvious antagonism she had toward him, Rick wanted to do the decent thing and at least apologise for the events of the previous night. But probably now was not quite the right time. Once in the safety of his home, Rick showered and changed.

The telephone rang. It was the hospital. More precisely it was Rachel Smithers. "Rick, you're back! Out of your ball and chains, eh? My God what a carry on! The cops obviously relented. There has been a huge furore at the hospital - they're all for you Rick. Even Rawarse got on the phone by his sick bed on CCU to rant and rave at the police." There was an excitement to her voice with more than a hint of admiration for her senior registrar. "We couldn't believe that you actually fought with your neighbour and then nicked her car to get to the hospital. Bloody hell, that's what I call dedication beyond the call of duty!" Rachel caught her breath before garrulously continuing on. "But I have to say that I for one am eternally grateful that you did. Do you know, Rick Donovan, that patient would be pushing up the daisies by now if you hadn't pitched up when you did. She owes you her life and I owe you my career."

"Well thank you ma'am, nice to know that I've got a few friends in various places. How is she doing by the way?" Rick enquired.

"If you mean Miss Belinda Jones, she's absolutely fine. I saw her this morning and she's going great guns. The anaesthetists have extubated her and she is now off the critical list. Obviously, she is not quite with it yet, but when she is, I bet she'll be asking after the suave young surgeon who saved her life. I don't think I'd have the heart to tell her that her saviour subsequently got banged up for beating up an old lady and car theft!" Rachel chuckled.

"Thanks a lot you cheeky, young pup. I shall treat that comment with the contempt it deserves. But tell me how's everything else? What with me being a jailbird and Rawarse being incarcerated in CCU there's not a lot of senior cover right now. Any problems on the wards or otherwise?"

"Well, now you mention it Rick, there is one problem I need to sort out. Let me see. Um… I'm going to book a table at Pavaronis tonight, but I am not sure whether to book it for one or for two. What do you suggest?"

There was a pause before Rick answered his SHO. "Dr Smithers, are you asking me out on a dinner date?"

"I might be."

"In that case book the table for two and be warned I have a voracious appetite."

"Sounds fun, and is your appetite merely of a gustatory nature?"

"That all depends what's on the menu." Rachel laughed and then told Rick that she would pick him up at 8 p.m. that evening. He protested that he was a male chauvinist and that he would pick her up at 7.30 p.m. before remembering that his car had been stolen and that if he did so, he would be forced to borrow Enid's Mini again.

"Ok, ok, you win. See you at eight o'clock. I'll be in my best bib and tucker waiting for you." Rick put the phone down and no sooner had he done so then the confounded thing rang again. The voice at the other end was in stark contrast to Rachel's jovial tone.

"Hello, is that Dr Donovan?"

"Speaking."

"Ah, Dr Donovan, my name is Andrew Kurfew. I work for the Hospital Trust in the personnel department."

"Oh yes." Rick had a fairly good idea what was coming.

"I'm afraid you've been suspended pending further enquiries into your behaviour following the events that have occurred over the last few days."

"Well thank you for breaking it so gently to me, and I have to say that I'm delighted to find the management are, as usual, being so supportive. Presumably you are still going to pay me, or will I be forced to go and beat up another old lady and steal her purse this time?"

"There is no need to be like that Dr Donovan. You have to understand the Trust's position…"

Rick interrupted the dry, unemotional voice of his pen-pushing colleague and forced himself to be civil. There was no point in being unnecessarily antagonistic. "That's fine. No doubt I'll hear from you in the near future regarding my forthcoming disciplinary hearing."

The personnel officer stuttered with surprise at the surgeon's forthright manner. "Well, err, yes I suppose that is the case. It also depends on the outcome of any police enquiries into the incident."

"Fine thanks for letting me know. Goodbye." Rick quickly put down the phone before there was any response and then unplugged the telephone lead from the socket.

'Bugger them,' he thought to himself. It was Rick's considered opinion that many in management really didn't know their arse from their elbow. He smiled to himself when he recalled Rawarse ranting and raving at different personnel managers about their ineptitude and loss of contact with the reality regarding ward life. Certainly many seemed to have a very limited idea of what really went on in the lives of the doctors and nurses they 'managed', and even less of an idea of the patients coming through their medical establishments. Sitting in their ivory towers, pens poised, they seemed miles away from the pain, the fear, the blood, vomit and faeces of the patients. They seemed just as far removed from the medical staff doing their best for the patients with limited resources and inadequate numbers. Rick stopped himself, he was angry but he couldn't tar all his managerial colleagues with the same brush. There were a few well-motivated individuals who truly understood that patients, and the doctors looking after them, were people, human beings with thoughts, fears, questions and emotions, not a number on a waiting list. There were those who acknowledged and understood the stresses of medics who operated at three in the morning to save a life, when their managerial colleagues were tucked up in bed and snoring. It was obvious that in the clinical areas where managers such as these worked and were supportive, patients were extremely well looked after, and there was satisfaction and harmony among clinical and non-clinical colleagues. However, it was already Rick's considered opinion that Andrew Kurfew was not such a manager.

The young gynaecologist turned his attention to matters closer to home. He felt obliged to at least apologise to his unfortunate next door neighbour. Perhaps if he could just explain to her the necessity for his actions and the sequel to them, she would understand and even forgive him. He donned his jacket and, closing his front door quietly, strolled down the cobbled street, crossed the road, and walked three blocks further on until he arrived at his local corner shop. There he bade the shop proprietor, a Mr Ivan Patel, a very good afternoon. Whenever Rick used the little corner shop, Mr Patel would always beam an ingratiating smile that made Rick feel slightly uneasy. Matters had progressed ever since Rick had safely delivered Mr Patel's fifth child. For a month afterwards, anything that Rick attempted to buy from the shop was lovingly wrapped and given to him free of charge, so much so that Rick became embarrassed by such generosity. In fact, Rick had had to stop shopping there for a while. Six months later and the free shopping had thankfully come to an end, but Mrs Patel was again with child and Rick feared that the whole episode would repeat itself. He placed a huge bouquet of flowers, a packet of Doggie Chocs, and a quarter bottle of best Russian vodka into the shopping basket. Rick had decided on flowers for Enid, Doggie Chocs for Mollie, and a quarter bottle of vodka for himself - a courage booster before seeking reconciliation.

Gossip surrounding the events of the preceding evening had spread like wildfire around the small local community and when Rick reached the cash register, Ivan smiled at him obsequiously. The shopkeeper, who also had first-hand experience of Enid and her mutt, took the quarter bottle of vodka out of the shopping basket and replaced it with a half bottle whilst muttering, "No extra charge Doctor, I think you'll need more than a quarter bottle." Ivan then chortled to himself, his grin widening as Rick thanked him and headed for the door. "Oh and Doctor, my wife and I... we will see you soon at the hospital...

yes?" Ivan looked over in the direction of his pregnant wife and raised his eyebrows.

Rick returned the shopkeeper's grin with a genuine smile of his own, and replied, "Of course Mr Patel, it would be an honour and a privilege to be of service again. And thank you for the Vodka....I think I am going to need it!"

As Rick exited the corner shop, as if like clockwork the heavens opened for the second time that day and Rick was soaked to the skin yet again. Cursing the British weather, he stomped home in the pouring rain, but was beginning to feel more like a bloody duck than a human being. On arriving home, Rick opened the vodka and poured himself a triple. He knew from past experience that vodka was an excellent alcoholic beverage if you didn't want anyone to know you'd been drinking. One's breath remained untainted but one's mind was made suitably uninhibited, which meant that fraught nerves were soon steadied. After changing out of his wet clothes, he waited a further twenty minutes or so for a good effect and then, summoning all his courage, picked up the flowers and the Doggie Chocs and made his way to Enid's front door. At least the rain had stopped. As he rang the bell he could feel his anxiety rising. 'Shit, I should have had more vodka,' he thought to himself, but it was too late. The front door slowly opened and there before him stood Enid Jones with her wretched hound yapping beside her.

"Um, err, Miss Jones. I… um… came over to apologise for last night and say how sorry I am," he stuttered nervously. The old lady looked him straight in the eye with utter, undisguised contempt. Rick forced his hand containing the flowers forward to within reach of the old woman. "Please forgive me, I did not mean you any harm." Enid took the flowers but remained absolutely silent. So Rick, despite feeling an unhealthy foreboding about his immediate future, spoke again. "And here, I thought Molly might like these."

As the medic nervously leant over to show the Doggie Chocs to Mollie, the little dog growled bearing her gleaming white canines threateningly. Rick fumbled with the packaging trying to open the box, in the vain hope that presenting the little dog with an actual edible treat would lead to the quiescence of her current aggressive demeanour. But disaster was to strike. Enid's front path was as slippery as an ice skating rink, courtesy of the recent downpour. The Vodka didn't help as Rick wobbled and then slipped down on his haunches, overbalanced and fell headlong into Enid's not so voluptuous bosom. Enid shrieked with startled surprise, as did Rick.

The little canine sensing her mistress to be under attack launched herself in the direction of Rick's more than slightly vulnerable crotch. The young surgeon was initially too stunned to think about evasive action, but the flash of white canines heading on a direct trajectory for his balls made his spinal cord kick into a spasm of natural reflexes, culminating in a 180 degree full body turn. The little dog's razor sharp teeth sunk themselves through Rick's clothing and on into the white flesh of his trembling arse. Needless to say, Rick, having already dropped the contents of the box of Doggie Chocs on Enid's front path, ran with some haste towards his objectionable neighbour's front gate, screaming in agony as he did so. Mollie, true to her breed, held on as if her very life depended upon it. She closed her eyes and concentrated on keeping her jaws firmly clamped shut as her whole body swung to the left and then the right, bouncing off Rick's battered buttocks as he strove forward.

Such a frenzy of activity brought with it the attention of many of the neighbours, whose net curtains now twitched at a record-breaking frequency. Windows started to open and the residents of the street started an impromptu cheer and laughter. It was the second time in two consecutive days that the street's entertainment had been provided by the old pensioner, her dog and the medic.

When Rick reached the gate, he heard Enid's shrill voice commanding her little dog to retreat. The jaws that clamped his buttocks with such a vice like grip released their hold, and Mollie scampered back up the path and into the safety of her home. She then turned to face her foe, yapping with as much ferociousness as a pint-size mutt could muster. Rick, clutching his rather painful arse, looked up at his neighbour from hell to see a smile widening on her wrinkled old face. He was too shocked to say anything, but just gazed in disbelief. Enid's eyes narrowed and she opened her mouth to speak. "Well, there's some justice at least, but if you think that I'm dropping police charges against you, you poor excuse for a young man, you are very much mistaken." She spat out the words with frightening venom before slamming her front door, taking the bouquet of flowers with her.

CHAPTER 10

Rick Donovan spent the remainder of the afternoon in his bathroom. Having struggled up the stairs, he dropped his trousers and boxers and, after placing a bathroom mirror just below waist level, studiously inspected his backside for any signs of damage. There were four teeth marks to be found on the inner aspect of Rick's right cheek, and by the look of them at least two had punctured the skin. "Sodding dog! Bloody bitch!" he murmured to himself as he gingerly applied cotton wool balls soaked in antiseptic to his increasingly painful wounds. He grimaced as the antiseptic started to sting, and it felt as if his whole bum was on fire. He silenced himself from gasping or crying out. He wasn't about to give the old bag next door any further gratification by letting her hear he was in agony. Having cleaned and dressed the bite wounds on his bottom, Rick made his way downstairs and found some antibiotics and analgesics that he kept in case of any emergencies and swallowed them with a glass of water. He was in two minds as to what he should do. He could call the police and inform them a vicious dog that happened to live next door had just attacked him, then he thought again. He could just imagine the police response, "So tell me sir, where exactly did the dog bite you? I see sir. Was it a big dog sir, a German Shepherd or a Rhodesian Ridgeback, for example? Oh, I see sir, a very small dog but very violent none the less. Right you are sir. And have you done anything recently to aggravate the dog's owner or the dog itself? You were what sir? Involved in a scuffle with your geriatric neighbour in which you revealed her baldness to the world before finally stealing her car. I see sir, and was this recently sir? Last night, umm, very good sir."

Rick decided against informing anyone, let alone the police. Instead he poured himself a large scotch, and lay on his stomach on the sofa and waited for the combination of alcohol and analgesic to work their magic. He contemplated the fact it was going to be extremely difficult to sit down for a few days, let alone have a decent crap – he'd be hovering over the loo for some time to come. Four large whiskies later, Rick found some relief from his aching backside in somnolence, although even in sleep he would shift uncomfortably one way then other. Once he rolled over onto his back and any pleasant dreams he was experiencing were brought to an abrupt end as the throbbing nature of his predicament was once again forced home. The evening arrived and Rick stirred to the sound of his front door bell. He carefully manoeuvred himself off the sofa and walked awkwardly through to the hall. He looked through the spy hole to distinguish friend from foe and was relieved to see Rachel and no one else. He opened the door and greeted his colleague with a beaming smile.

"Rachel, hi, you're a sight for sore eyes. Come on in. How are you doing?" Rick just about managed to stop himself from slurring his words. He leant forward and kissed Rachel gently on the cheek. She responded with a cheeky grin and in turn kissed Rick on his other cheek, continental style.

"It's French night tonight is it?" Her eyes sparkled with a mischievous twinkle. "Oh and I'm fine, thank you. How was your first day of freedom?"

Rick led her down the hall and into the kitchen. "Well, I have to say that I would probably have had a better day if I had thrown myself stark-bollock naked into a tank of ravenous piranhas."

"Like that was it?" Rachel could not help but

smirk. "So are you going to tell me all about it?"

"Glass of wine?" he offered.

"Absolutely, thank you."

Rick opened a bottle of Chardonnay and poured out two rather large glasses of the chilled wine. He passed one of them to Rachel and held his glass up. "Cheers Rachel, nice to have you in my humble abode. Now let me see. As to why it has not been the best of days. Um…to put it bluntly, I spent the morning in a police cell, was suspended by our dear management colleagues at the hospital, failed in my efforts as a diplomat and darn well nearly lost my testicles to the dog next door. I don't think it gets any better than that, do you?"

"Oh Rick, you poor old darling. No wonder you are half-pickled already. I did notice that you are walking rather oddly. So where did the dog get you - or more to the point, are your testicles still intact?" Rachel looked so earnest and asked with such sincerity about his nether regions that Rick couldn't help but smile. She immediately picked up on his amusement and the funny side of Rick's experience became apparent. They refilled their glasses, laughing as they did so and the atmosphere became charged with hilarity and mirth. Rick only hoped that Enid could hear them. He told Rachel the whole story of his miserable day, from Ivan the corner shop proprietor to that little shit of a dog, next door and his equally turd-like mistress. They quickly finished the first bottle of wine and as inhibitions sunk away the laughter and chortling got progressively louder. They decided that as Rick could hardly sit down, a meal at a restaurant was probably not such a good idea. Rick telephoned for an Indian takeaway, lit a real fire in the lounge and opened another bottle of wine. Rachel consoled him that at least his balls hadn't been chewed. Later on, well into the evening after they had eaten, Rick was so relaxed he even temporarily forgot about his bottom, until he sat on it, that is. He responded with lightning reflexes and after the pain had subsided they both collapsed with laughter onto the floor of the lounge, Rick admittedly into a prone position.

"Rick have you had anyone look at the dog bites?" Rachel chuckled.

"Ah yes. I spent a good deal of the afternoon inspecting my derriere in the bathroom mirror and what a fine pair of buttocks I possess, although now horribly blemished by that mutt next door. Never again will I be able to moon with pride on a drunken night out."

"I trust you've cleaned it properly, Dr Donovan? It wouldn't be very nice getting an infection in that area and your mooning days would then definitely be over forever. Why don't you let me have a peep, just to make sure? From a purely medical point of view, you understand."

The booze was by now having a deleterious effect on their functioning brain cells and they were both pretty far gone. "Well just a quick glimpse then," Rick slurred, and with that he stood up, slightly dropped his trousers and boxers so that only the top of his buttocks could be visualised.

"Oh come now Dr Donovan, stop being so modest. I need to have a really good look." With that Rachel gently took hold of his trousers and boxers and eased them down. Rick did not try and stop her and his clothes fell around his ankles. He stepped out of them to avoid tripping up and Rachel placed her hands on his naked buttocks, looking at the dog bites as she did so. "Excellent job Rick, the wounds certainly look clean. Are you taking antibiotics just in case?" Rachel noticed the almost inaudible gasp as she touched him. She smiled to herself. Then, ever so slowly moved her hands over his skin and around to his hips.

"Rachel what are you doing?" Rick whispered, but they both knew exactly what she was doing and where it would it would lead. Her hands stirred inwards and downwards to the tops of his inner thighs. He angled his body, straining towards her. Rick shuddered, and knew then that he wanted her. He wanted the comfort of human flesh and he needed to release all the pent-up emotions and frustrations of the last few days. He turned to face her, her hands remaining on his body as he rotated around. She stood up straight and kissed him lightly on the mouth, whilst her hands tenderly slid towards his manhood. Their lips opened and he found heaven in the soft, wet, abundant flesh of her mouth. Rick found the zip at the back of her dress and while they tasted the intimacy of each other's tongues and mouths, he disrobed her, his hands smoothly running down her spine, massaging her, delighting in the silky texture of her skin. They both stood naked in front of the fire, touching, nibbling, and tenderly kissing. The tension then increased wonderfully into a crescendo of vocal disinhibition and frantic activity. In the physical and emotional frenzy to get at each other, they accidentally pushed over a single leg ornamental table and the wine and glasses went tumbling. Rick gently pulled away from her for just for a few seconds.

"Forget it," he whispered, staring straight into her eyes. He then held her at arm's-length and just looked, feasting on her sumptuous female form. He was as hard as a granite pillar, and she was wet from wanting him.

She smiled. "You go on top - we've got to protect those sore buttocks, after all." They both laughed and eased themselves onto the rug, Rachel beneath him. The log fire crackled and various artists crooned out their love songs on the CD player, but all such sounds were drowned out by the ferocity and intensity of their blissfully physical lovemaking.

Enid was in bed with a cup of cocoa when the noises from next door started. Molly, who was lying faithfully as ever on the floor beside the bed, looked up at her mistress anxiously. Enid had gone to bed particularly pleased with the events of the day. She had sought and gained at least some degree of retribution from her enemy neighbour and now the bastard at least had something to remember her by. Perhaps next time he would think before attacking a little old defenceless pensioner. However, the evening had soured her pleasure somewhat when initially she had heard tittering and then laughter coming through the wall. There was no mistaking his dulcet tones, but there was also a softer female voice. How could he be in there, laughing and enjoying himself after everything that had happened over the previous two days? But then the noises had turned from laughter to various gasping and grunting expletives that filtered straight up the chimney and through the brickwork to bombard Enid's good ear. The old lady heard the sound of breaking glass as if something had been pushed off a table top. It was then that she started to worry. With the memory of her struggle with the brute still burning fresh on her memory, her mind started to conjure up all sorts of horrible pictures. Rick definitely had a young woman in there, probably innocent and unable to defend herself. What if he had been trying to force himself on her and she had struggled to become free? Enid knew in her own mind what a monster he was. After all, she had only last night experienced his devilish ways. Various moans then echoed through the wall, becoming louder and louder, almost rhythmical until the young girl screamed, obviously in agony. Enid swore she could even hear the breathing of his prey becoming faster and louder as the bastard tortured her.

The old lady could take it no longer. She picked up the phone and dialled 999.

"Hello, what service do you require?" a female monotone voice warbled.

"Police please, and quickly young lady. Hello… is that the police… oh thank God… please you must come as fast as you can. There's a young girl next door. She's being tortured. I've heard the sound of shattered glass and screams for him to stop whatever it is that he is doing. She might be dead by now. Do you hear me? You must come immediately." After informing the startled police officer of the exact address to which she was referring, Enid put down the phone, and breathed a sigh of relief that she had been instrumental in the cessation of a great harm.

The tone and urgency of the old woman's voice prompted the policewoman at the switchboard to take immediate action. An operational panda car was immediately summoned with blue light to the address given. Furthermore instructions were given that speed was of the utmost importance and the officers responding to the call were given permission to force entry onto the premises if necessary. After all, a young girl's life was at stake. Roger and Dave were parked up in a layby finishing off their Beef Burgers when the call came through. The inside of the panda car resembled a badly maintained Fast Food Restaurant with wrappers and empty cartons strewn across the dashboard and the back seat. Dave wiped away a remnant of sauce that had dribbled from his chops and turned to his partner. "Aw, bloody 'ell, there's no time in the day to enjoy your food anymore. Rush, bloody rush," he slobbered. Roger threw his eyes heavenward in agreement with his colleague, and belched. Heaving an enormous sigh, he started up the *BMW*'s powerful engine and clicked the automatic gearbox into drive.

"Hang on a second... Dave, that address, does it ring any bells for you?"

"Yeah, now you come to mention it, isn't that address in the vicinity of that old witch? You know the one whose car got nicked by that doctor bloke?"

"You're right. In fact isn't that the address of the doctor we banged up last night?"

"Bloody 'ell, I thought he was all right. Perhaps looks are a bit deceiving. Who knows, maybe he beats up old ladies one night, then goes in for a bit of rape and pillage the next."

The panda car pulled up outside Rick's house. The couple inside were oblivious to the flashing lights and the sound of a siren. The policemen rang the doorbell several times, but Rick and Rachel were deaf to all and everything other than their own physical pleasure. Acting on their previous instructions Roger and Dave forced the front door and flew into the lounge to be greeted by the sight of Rick's heaving buttocks.

The police officers both stopped dead in their tracks. From what they could see it certainly did not look as if a young woman had been coerced in any way, in fact judging by the marks on Dr Donovan's bottom, it was he who needed protection from her razor sharp nails. Rachel looked up in horror at the two policemen, who she recognised from the previous night. They just stood red-faced in the doorway, immobile with shock, witnessing what should have been a very private act.

"Oh Bollocks," the two coppers said in unison.

Rick arched around, pulling away from his beloved and nearly castrating himself in the process. There followed a moment of incredulous silence, before Rachel screamed at the astounded police officers.

"What the friggin' hell do you think you are doing, you bloody perverts? Get out! Get out! Do you hear me?"

"Um, you're not hurt then, you're OK?" Roger trembled.

"OK? Not hurt? You stupid bloody idiot! You burst into a private house and stand there gawking like a couple of peeping toms while a couple are trying to make love. Yes, Officer, I'm just bloody perfect, thanks for dropping in. Now piss off before I call the real police." Rachel grabbed her discarded dress and held it to her chest, hiding her breasts from the officers' glare. Both Dave and Roger, realising they had made a terrible mistake, backed out of the room, averting their eyes as they did so.

"Um, err, w-w-we are very, very sorry Sir and Madam, but we were given information that led us to believe someone was being hurt." Dave spoke as if he were a chastised child seeking atonement for a wrongdoing.

"Let me guess," Rick was thoroughly pissed off by now. "It was that bloody woman next door again." His anger was starting to rise. Roger and Dave sensing that that they were on risky ground made a hasty retreat. They almost ran from the room, stumbling over each other in their attempts to exit. "We'll obviously make good any damage to your house and again many apologies for disturbing you," Roger shouted before closing the battered front door behind him. Enid's curtain twitched as she despondently observed the policemen leaving the scene of the crime without so much as a handcuffed ruffian. The lovers looked to the closed door and then at each other. Rachel suddenly started to laugh and Rick looked on in amazement. "Rachel, what on earth is so funny?"

"You and what you said earlier."

"What for goodness sake?"

"That your mooning days were well and truly over."

"Sorry?"

"Oh Rick, that was probably the best moon you've ever done, and to a couple of coppers at that." The tense atmosphere, which had been strained almost to breaking point, lifted. Rick looked at his lover, and she at him. Once again they laughed, and melting into each other's arms, made love for the second time that night.

CHAPTER 11

The Intensive Care Unit buzzed with a frenzy of high-tech activity and staff hurried here and there. The sound of computerised blood pressure monitors, combined with the blips, the bleeps, and tens of different warning alarm systems associated with ventilators, ECG displays and oxygen saturation equipment, filled the air. Amid each unconscious person's life form ran a series of tubes, catheters, drains, and electronic gadgetry that made the human being lying there look almost robotic. A screen above each bed flickered with an array of information that told a passing medic all he could wish to know of that patient's physical state. Occasionally a groan from the unfortunates who happened to be in such a predicament could be heard, but in the main the patients were far too sick to make any noise - at least, any sound that was audible above the cacophony of technology. Into this strange and unreal atmosphere in which fifty per cent of patients headed heavenward, Belinda Jones regained a semblance of consciousness. She had been there for nearly two days, with no recollection of anything since painfully crawling through her apartment to her telephone, to make that lifesaving call. She ached all over, particularly in her abdomen. But the pain, that terrible piercing pain in her pelvis, had gone. Her vision was hazy and her senses confused at the bombardment of strange sights and sounds. The alien smell of hospital disinfectants further perplexed her battling senses. She tried to swallow and her throat felt like it had been cut, the result of the breathing tube that had only recently been removed. A blood pressure cuff started to inflate around her arm automatically and pinched her skin as it did so. She looked down at her arm to see a number of tubes trailing from her veins. She tried to move but was too weak. Belinda opened her mouth to speak but could only manage a whisper..

On the far side of the room, there was a flurry of concentrated activity. People were running in and out from behind a set of curtains. Shouts of, "Stand clear, defibrillating now!" were heard echoing around the room and then as fast as it all began the commotion ceased. A little while later, out of the corner of her blurred vision, Belinda saw two men go behind the curtain with what looked like a coffin on wheels. They exited silently and were gone with the body of the poor soul who had just died. Within twenty minutes, another person was occupying that same bed. Then fear came to Belinda and the realisation of her own mortality. She had just witnessed the death of some poor unfortunate individual. A human being, a character, someone with thoughts and feelings, aspirations, family and friends, who had been lying in a bed not fifteen yards from where she lay, and had now just gone to meet his or her maker. She yearned for someone to talk to, someone who could reassure her and just say that everything would be all right, but no one came. She tried to call out once again but to no avail and, exhausted with her efforts, yet still terrified, she drifted back into a disturbed and uncomfortable sleep.

An hour or so later, she was roused once more by the weeping of a woman, crying for her daughter in the bed adjacent to Belinda's own. The distress of the woman heightened Belinda's sense of fear and alarm. Lying in that bed on the Intensive Care Unit she came close to what could only be described as a panic attack. Thoughts of death, of being wheeled out of the place in that coffin on wheels, took an irrational hold of her mind and she prayed for some kind of deliverance. Her eyes filled with tears, and she started to shake uncontrollably, becoming desperate, and then God answered her prayers.

The stranger arrived and with a look of concern he studied the electronic screen at the top end of her bed, checked her charts and then seated himself on a stool to one side of where she lay. Belinda knew she had never seen him before, yet in a bizarre way she thought she recognised him. He saw her searching eyes and smiled at her. He seemed to perceive the terror in her expression and understood immediately the content of her thoughts. When their eyes met, their minds quite simply connected. As he sat by her bed, he gently took and held her hand, softly whispering reassuring words to her about how she had been seriously ill and needed an operation, but that now everything was fine, and she just needed to get stronger. With his arrival, she knew she was not going to die and she knew that this man was responsible for saving her life. He sat with her for no more than two to three minutes and then was gone, but her morbid thoughts had been vanquished and her mood lifted. She saw him having a word with a nurse before disappearing and it was evidently concerning her welfare. It was ridiculous but she mourned his going, and then found herself eagerly awaiting his return. He did not return that day, but Belinda had another visitor later on in the afternoon.

Enid had received two telephone calls that morning. One was from the police asking the pensioner to confirm the recovery of her delivered *Mini* and secondly to accuse and caution her of wasting police time, in addition to potentially causing havoc in the force's relationship with the local community. Sergeant Dulwit was particularly scathing about Miss Jones interpreting the sound of innocent lovemaking for cold-blooded murder, and was even more exasperated that the local police force were now in danger of being labelled as peeping perverts. After warning the old woman not to repeat such aberrant reporting, Dulwit rang off. Enid had remained uncharacteristically quiet.

The second telephone call was from the local hospital. A woman by the name of Mrs Churchill told Enid that she was a liaison administrator in charge of patients' relatives and that Enid was not to worry. Prior to the damn woman telling her not to worry, Enid had not. But there was obviously some sort of bad news and having been informed she must not worry, reverse psychology took its toll and Enid suddenly became sick with anxiety. The hospital administrator persisted in trying to appease Enid into not worrying, without telling why it was that she had been contacted.

"Now look here Mrs Churchill, instead of telling me not to worry just bloody well tell me what it is that I do not have to worry about."

"Really, Mrs Jones, I can reassure you that the worst is now over and that everything will be fine."

"Look you stupid woman! Will you just please tell me what has happened. For God's sake spit it out!"

Finally, Mrs Churchill told Enid that a young woman who they believed to be her niece had undergone emergency surgery. She was now on the Intensive Care Unit, and that Enid was not to worry because her niece was now off the danger list and soon to be returned to the ward. Enid was stunned into silence. After the death of Belinda's parents in a car crash some years previously she had tried to be like a mother to the girl, and as such she was now her next of kin. Despite the fact that the two of them did not always see eye to eye, Belinda was her favourite niece and in fact she was the only one to ever visit Enid or take an interest in her. The thought of her lying in a hospital bed in the Intensive Care Unit filled the old woman with horror.

"I must visit her immediately. My God, she needs me now above all times," Enid murmured to herself. "Um, thank you Mrs Churchill, I will of course be up to see my niece this afternoon. She is all right though - she is not in any immediate danger?"

"No, Miss Jones. I am reliably informed that your niece is off the critical list and her condition is now quite stable."

"The critical list, do you mean she nearly died?" Enid retorted.

Mrs Churchill shifted uncomfortably in her seat and Enid could sense the tension in her voice. "Yes Miss Jones, she was a very sick woman and needed emergency surgery, but I repeat, she is stable now. The surgeon who operated has been to see her this morning and is happy that she is progressing well and is in no danger of relapsing. In fact, tomorrow he intends to transfer her to the general ward."

Enid felt a sudden and almost overwhelming gratitude to the hospital staff who had saved her niece's life and softened her tone towards the administrator who had initially irritated her. "God bless the man who saved my Belinda's life," she whispered to herself and, thanking Mrs Churchill, rang off.

It was about three o'clock in the afternoon when the old lady tentatively drove to the hospital in her beloved old Mini. She sat as upright in the driving seat as her distorted kyphotic back would allow. Her face was just about visible over the steering wheel, which her wrinkly, thin fingers grasped. Her eyesight was not as good as it had once been, and instead of using perfectly serviceable indicators, Enid utilised old fashioned hand signals that were unrecognisable to any other driver on the road. Needless to say, she left a trail of chaos and some very red faces in her wake. Fortunately, the majority of other drivers on the road that afternoon, seeing and realising it was an old dear who had just cut them up, were inclined to excuse her inept driving skills. Even the police seemed to take a lenient stand on the matter.

Dave and Roger were travelling along the high street at a law abiding thirty miles an hour, when from out of a side street screeched a battered old Mini directly in their path. Roger swerved the big panda car out of the way, narrowly missing an oncoming motorist as he did so. He slammed on the *BMW*'s brakes, the ABS took over and a major accident was averted. The driver in the oncoming car blasted his horn and rotated a single finger suggestively at the two police officers. "Swivel on that you bastards!" he shouted angrily from his open window before driving off in disgust.

Roger and Dave were initially too stunned to react to the insult and by the time they had regained their composure he was long gone. But Dave at least had feelings regarding the driver of the Mini. "That bloody *Mini*, come on Rog, put on the blue light. Let's get the sod for dangerous driving."

"Um, well I'm not sure that is such a good idea Dave. Did you see who was driving?"

"Some bloody maniac I presume."

"Well, try Enid Jones." As Roger said the name, all desire for revenge or retribution instantly disappeared from Dave's mind. The thought of another confrontation with the old witch was more than he could bear. The panda car turned around and headed off in the direction of the nearest Pizza parlour. Enid continued her route to the hospital, causing havoc on Cardiff's roads as she did so. Fortunately, as luck would have it, there were no major pile-ups or casualties, although there was no shortage of faces flushed red with rage, fists shaken out of car windows, and the almost inevitable swearing at the old lady for her driving misdemeanours.

The gentle cold touch of Enid's wrinkled hand on her own awoke Belinda from her slumber. She opened her eyes to see her aged aunt sitting beside her bed in the Intensive Care Unit, with a concerned smile on her worried and frowning face. Belinda could see that those very same smiling eyes betrayed a look of deep concern and the young woman, true to her nature, automatically attempted to alleviate any worry that her Aunt Enid felt.

"My dear Aunt Enid, you must not worry. I will soon be out of here," she whispered, gently squeezing the old lady's hand.

"Shhhh, my child, don't use up your valuable energy trying to comfort me, you are the one who needs comforting and support, not me." Enid reached out and with her other hand tenderly stroked the young woman's forehead. It was not long before Belinda was asleep again. Enid stayed with her for the remainder of the afternoon, holding her hand and stroking her forehead and cheeks, whispering words of reassurance to her. She even prayed over her niece, asking for God to give her back the strength of youth and promote a speedy recovery. The old woman showed a completely different side to her character.

She felt a real need to care. The young woman who lay before her was probably the only other creature in the world - apart from Molly, of course - who had ever really shown her any real love. As early evening came, although it was difficult to ascertain what time of day it was in the ICU, Enid thought of her little dog cooped up in the house all afternoon. She probably needed a pee. Enid sighed and got up from her chair. She kissed her niece fondly on the cheek and spoke softly into her ear. "I'll be back in the morning my dear. You just get yourself better."

Before she left, Enid Jones sought out the nurse in charge of her niece's care. She thanked her effusively for looking after Belinda and asked her to relay her gratitude to the surgeon who had saved her niece's life. She also asked why it was that her niece had been taken so ill. The nurse replied that a blood vessel in her abdomen had ruptured and that Belinda had lost an enormous quantity of blood. Fortunately, the nurse maintained medical confidentiality, and Enid never found out that Belinda had been pregnant. The staff nurse went on to reassure Enid that her niece was doing exceptionally well following surgery. She was confident Belinda would be well enough to be transferred off ICU to the gynaecology ward the following morning and she kindly gave Enid instructions on how to get to the gynaecology ward, if she wished to visit her niece the following day.

"Bless you dear and bless the medical staff who saved my Belinda," Enid smiled at the nurse and then sauntered out of the hospital. Once she had found her little car, she jumped in and started it up, then driving like a maniac out of the hospital main entrance, she nearly ran over a rather shocked car park attendant who was busy ticketing a double parked car. As the unfortunate man dived for cover, he pushed over an overflowing rubbish bin and ended up wallowing around in putrefying refuse. He sat with a banana skin on his head in utter disbelief as Enid drove past. The odoriferous fellow looked on in fury and opened his mouth to shout abuse. But Enid merely smiled and waved at him. She was not in a cantankerous mood. After all, the good Lord had just saved her niece from the jaws of death. The old age pensioner drove past the bewildered attendant and then home to a little terrace house on one of the many cobbled streets of Cardiff.

CHAPTER 12

Rick was in the bathtub when the telephone rang. He was bathing the dog bites on his aching bum with diluted antiseptic water. He carefully manoeuvred himself out of the bath, wrapped a towel around his midriff and hobbling into the hall, picked up the phone. "Hello!" He barked down the line, displeased at having to rush his ablutions.

"Oh, um, hello, is that Dr Donovan?" a rather nervous male voice asked.

"Yes this is Rick Donovan, how can I help you?" Rick recognised the voice but could not quite place it.

"Ah, Dr Donovan, you may remember me; we spoke on the telephone yesterday. Andrew Kurfew here from administration... at the hospital."

There was a short awkward pause while Rick racked his brains as to why the management would be calling him at home again. Perhaps it was because he had visited the hospital that morning to check on the ward patients and Belinda Jones in particular. He decided that the best form of defence was to go on the offensive and, gripping the receiver, he did his best to rant down the telephone. "Oh for God's sake, you haven't phoned me because of this morning? I only stepped into the hospital because I wanted to see if Miss Jones was progressing OK following surgery. Is that a crime? Let me guess, I am banned forthwith from trespassing on hospital premises, hospital grounds or within five miles of the hospital perimeter, on pain of death and being duffed up by hospital security."

Andrew Kurfew quickly intervened whilst Rick drew breath. "Dr Donovan, please calm yourself. That is not the case at all, in fact it is to be commended that you were concerned enough about your patients to want to review them, particularly the young lady in question who I have been informed was very ill, but is now making a good recovery… thanks to you."

"Well I'm relieved to hear that at least. So how else might I have offended the mighty wheels of administrative power?"

"Dr Donovan, you've offended no-one. In fact, I

am telephoning you because the hospital needs your help. It would appear that a flu epidemic has meant that three of the specialist registrars have unfortunately gone off ill, another is already on maternity leave and as you know Sir John Rawarse isn't in the best of health. To be frank that leaves us with a serious staff shortage."

Another, slightly longer pause followed. Rick was slightly bewildered. "Sorry, you want my help?" he asked incredulously. The tone of his voice changed from being aggressive to irritatingly smug. "Hang on a minute now. You want my help despite the fact that only yesterday the precious Hospital Trust shafted me, and you yourself informed that me that I was suspended until further notice?"

"Apologies but please understand, I was only doing my job, Dr Donovan. We were only acting to maintain the Hospital's good name; there is no vendetta against you personally." Mr Kurfew sounded suitably apologetic.

"So how come the powers that be think I'm unfit to work one day, then hey presto, I am suddenly the answer to their prayers the next?" Rick was interested to hear the response.

"Dr Donovan, it is the patients that must have the

priority in all this. Staffing levels are dangerously low. There has never been any question about your competence, just your means of getting to the hospital. Now please can you help us or not?"

"Well Mr Kurfew, that all depends whether you've lifted my suspension doesn't it?"

"Well, we are clearly lifting the suspension to enable you to come back...aren't we?"

"What about the disciplinary hearing? Rick enquired and then added while Kurfew hesitated, "And can you answer this..." there was a pause before Rick continued, "Where is the care for medical staff in all this? After taking major personal risks for the sake of our patients, in fact saving a young woman's life, and then being banged up in a Police cell, I am then phoned to be told that I am suspended by the very organisation that is meant to support me – what would the Trust have preferred - that I left that young woman to die?"

"Dr Donovan, you already know the answer to that, but I am afraid there will still need to be a disciplinary hearing, we can't change that."

"Well get yourself another medic then!" As Rick spoke he regretted it and realised there was little point in being unnecessarily antagonist. It was not professional, even if Kurfew was a twat. He retracted his statement. "Oh listen, I apologise, it's just the last few days have been a bit difficult." And then doing what medics always do, Rick agreed to help out, "Yes Mr Kurfew, I'll help out. See you first thing on Monday morning."

"Thank you for your co-operation, Dr Donovan, and just so you know this phone call has been duly recorded." There was a hint of a threatening tone in Mr Kurfew's voice, and Rick rightly or wrongly couldn't help but sense that Kurfew was not on his side. He put the phone down.

Monday came around too soon and Rick, cursing the fact that he was still without a car, stood at a bus stop in the pouring rain on a dull and overcast Cardiff morning. It was 7:30 a.m. and the young surgeon was not at his best, especially when the wind got up. A spectacularly strong gust caught his golfing umbrella and dragged him into the road and into the path of an oncoming car. The driver of the car swerved with exaggerated gusto and still managed to sound his horn and stick an offensive finger up at Rick as he sped on past through a deep, murky puddle that was churned up and flung in Rick's general direction. It was not a good start to the week.

A timeworn, unkempt woman also waiting for public transport cackled with delight at the young man's misfortune. "He got you good and proper, didn't he love?" she smirked as Rick returned to his place in the queue, her wrinkled old face distorted and sniggering. Rick ignored the old bag and prayed for the arrival of the blessed bus. It did finally turn up, 35 minutes late, by which time Rick was so cold and wet that he was visibly shaking. He wondered sometimes why anyone bothered going to work. Year in and year out, millions of people trudged to work on a Monday morning with a sense of dread and foreboding, a whole five days to go before the relief of the weekend. Then more often than not he was on call over Saturday and Sunday too. He finally arrived at the hospital and made his way up to the gynaecology ward where he was thankfully greeted by Rachel who, sensing that he had had a bad start, grabbed his arm and walked him into the staff coffee room.

"Good morning Mr Donovan. What a nice surprise to see you. I take it the management relented?"

"More like they were desperate and with no alternative."

"Well, I for one am very happy to see you." She raised an eyebrow provocatively then, leaning towards him, whispered, "How is your bottom this fine morning?"

The room was otherwise deserted and she reached up, planted her lips firmly over his mouth, and kissed him. "You looked as if you needed that," Rachel's big green eyes looked up at him flirtatiously. "Now shall we appease the management and go and see some patients."

After that, Rick's day seemed to get better. They carried out the ward round efficiently and professionally, reviewing the emergency patients from the night before: women who were bleeding, women who were miscarrying, women with pelvic pain, women who had slept with the wrong man and now suffered with pelvic infection and the possible prospect of future infertility. Rick dealt with them all effectively and with empathy, explaining the likely cause of their predicament and the investigations and management plan to be followed. It was turning out to be a nice but manic day, especially when Rick was asked to do Sir John Rawarse's theatre list as an extra. No one from the management team had cancelled the old man's operating list despite the fact the senior gynaecologist was unwell. Patients had come from far and wide, arranged time off from work, sorted out babysitters, and in some cases even cancelled holidays to be there for their operations. So the possibility of the list being cancelled was not one that was welcomed and the waiting pre-operative patients were ever so slightly relieved to see Mr Rick Donovan.

Rick and Rachel literally ran from one grateful patient to another as they explained and consented them for their operations, then after swallowing a sandwich in the corridor on the way to the gynaecology theatre, they started the surgical session. By the end of the afternoon, both were knackered but satisfied that their work was done.

As they walked out of the theatre suite and on to their gynaecology unit, Rick had a sudden realisation and turning to his senior house officer asked, "Rachel, we haven't seen Belinda Jones, I take it she is off ICU now and on the ward?"

"Yes she is off ICU and doing really well." Rachel guided him to a side room at the far end of the ward.

Rick knocked courteously on the door before entering the room. Belinda lay quietly on the hospital bed; her eyes were closed and she was sleeping. The drips had been removed from her arms, as well as all the high-tech paraphernalia that had surrounded her on the Intensive Care Unit. Rick stood in the doorway for a short time just looking at her. She was the most beautiful creature he had ever seen in his life. When he had reviewed her on the Intensive Care Unit he had experienced the oddest of feelings - pleasant feelings, he recalled. She had looked so frightened, and held onto his hand with such strength, he had wanted to comfort her. The strangest thing was that Rick Donovan felt a strange premonition that somehow this woman's destiny was inextricably tied up with his own.

Rachel shuffled uncomfortably. "Shall I wake her, Rick?"

"Oh, um yes of course. Thank you." Rachel went around to the right side of the bed and placed a hand on Belinda's shoulder and, shaking her gently, quietly spoke. "Belinda... Miss Jones... hello... we are the doctors looking after you... Belinda." Rachel gently shook the young woman's shoulder again and she awoke with a start.

The young woman initially looked up at Dr Rachel Smithers, but her gaze was soon diverted and it was Rick who now received her full attention. Belinda smiled the most beautiful of smiles unswervingly at him. There was no awkwardness or embarrassment as her eyes fixed on him and remained there. Rachel coughed as if to break the spell and as she opened her mouth to speak Belinda cut her off. "It was you who saved my life. You visited me on the Intensive Care Unit and you were wonderful. Thank you, doctor."

Rachel was about to throw up. Some appreciation was always very pleasant, but flagrant, grovelling gratitude was nauseating. Rick was in a trance-like state, bewildered by his strength of feeling for this woman. One thing was for sure, it had all been worth it. The stealing of Enid's car, the police chase, the night in a police cell, even his temporary suspension by the hospital trust; it had all been worth it to save this woman's life. Rick finally came to his senses and shook himself out of the spell she cast upon him.

"Miss Jones, it is all part of the job. I am just very pleased that you seem to be doing so well postoperatively." He returned her smile and, getting hold of his personal feelings once more, matter-of-factly continued with matters medical. He asked her how she was feeling, looked at her wound, checked her observations and ensured that her recovery was going to plan. He then sat on the bed next to her and explained all that had happened and why she had been so ill. He explained that one of her fallopian tubes had been removed, but that it was still possible to conceive with just one tube left. He then invited her to ask any questions and answered them fully and comprehensively. Throughout the bedside consultation, Belinda failed to detect any judgmental attitude about the fact that she was unmarried and she had been pregnant. The gynaecologist showed only concern for her welfare.

When the medical team finally left the side room to continue on their way, a full thirty minutes had elapsed and still Rick found himself not wanting to leave her. He chastised himself for being so ridiculous. "Rick, for God's sake, get a grip, you are her doctor," was the thought foremost in the young gynaecologist's mind. And with that he finally tore himself away.

As they exited from the room, Rachel spoke up. "Streuth Rick, that was a bit of a marathon wasn't it? I thought you were going put up a bloody camp bed and stay there all night." There was a hint of jealousy in her tone and Rachel remained quiet for the rest of the working day.

When the day was done, Rick was grateful to finally get home. He was appreciative of the fact that Rachel had offered him a lift and he hadn't had to rely on the Cardiff Bus service. When they arrived back at his little terraced house, he thanked Rachel and was not even aware of her disappointment when he failed to invite her in. He made himself a light supper, showered and went to bed, but all the time there were a series of thoughts that would just not leave him, and they were centred on a Miss Belinda Jones.

CHAPTER 13

Tuesday morning was always fertility clinic and Rick had always enjoyed this aspect of the job. He had learnt to his horror that one in six couples were unable to conceive naturally and he was only too pleased to be able to help them. Most couples were usually very supportive of each other, but Rick soon found that this trait was not universal. Furthermore, every now and again Rick was staggered by the ignorance of the occasional couple attending. That afternoon proved to be no exception. Rick called Mr and Mrs Whiplash into his consulting room. They sat down in front of him and Rick started the consultation.

"Well I am very pleased to be able to tell you that the results of the tests back so far are normal." Rick turned the notes on his desk around so that the couple could see written confirmation of what he was telling them, and then pointing a finger to the relevant test result continued. "Here is the result of your semen analysis, Mr Whiplash, and as you can see you appear to be firing on all cylinders."

Mr Whiplash puffed out his chest proudly before looking over to his anxious-looking wife.

Rick carried on. "The World Health Organisation states that a normal sperm count is 20 million of the little fellas per millilitre, and you sir have 60 million, most impressive."

Whiplash cut him short. "So I am a bit of a stud then?" he blurted out in a deep northern accent.

"Err… you could say that." Rick was slightly surprised.

"And that means it's not my fault we cannot have a baby. It's hers, isn't it?" The obnoxious man pointed an accusing finger at his long-suffering wife.

Mrs Whiplash turned a sickly shade of green; beads of sweat appeared on her forehead and she began to shake uncontrollably before eventually bursting into tears. Rick shuffled uncomfortably in his seat and tried to rectify the situation.

"Well actually, no Mr Whiplash; firstly I have to say that it really isn't terribly helpful to try and appoint blame in these matters, and secondly just because the number of sperms is OK doesn't necessarily mean they are capable of doing any fertilising." Rick passed the unfortunate woman a tissue. "Also I am pleased to say that all the tests done on you, Mrs Whiplash, have proved to be normal. You appear to be ovulating, your tubes are in good working order and your baseline hormones are all within the normal range."

Her husband for some bizarre reason was evidently displeased at Rick's remarks, and became more aggressive. "If you're so bloody clever with all your tests, Doctor, and everything is normal, why the bloody 'ell can't she get pregnant eh?"

Rick was about to inform Whiplash that approximately twenty percent of couples had what was called 'Unexplained Infertility' when Mrs Whiplash suddenly stood up and wiped her eyes dry. She looked down contemptuously at her husband, who looked as shocked as Rick felt, and calmly stated, "I've had enough of this bullshit", and then glaring at Mr Whiplash matter-of-factly stated, "And I've had enough of you."

Rick was by now, more than a little uncomfortable and had no desire to be an intermediary in what was fast becoming a heated marital dispute. But Mrs

Whiplash was not finished and Rick couldn't escape.

"Doctor, the reason I cannot get pregnant is that ninety nine percent of the time," and she pointed an accusatory finger at her husband, "he can't get it up. There's only so much a woman can do with a flaccid chipolata. The fact that he managed to give a sample at all is a bloody miracle - in fact, I wouldn't be surprised if it was someone else's sperm." With that Mrs Whiplash picked up her coat and headed for the door. As she exited she called back to her shaken partner, "Oh and by the way, I want a divorce. Now I am going to my mother's."

The door was slammed behind her and the worm had most definitely turned. The indignant woman's husband sat in stunned silence, Rick too was initially speechless. Then it was Whiplash's turn to cry. In a matter of seconds he turned from an aggressive man into a sobbing child. Great tears welled up in his eyes and rolled down his cheeks. Rick passed over the box of clinic tissues that was always on standby for such occasions and was alarmed at the rapid rate at which they diminished. Whiplash was by now almost inconsolable. Rick was feeling sorry for the fellow, after all impotence was a dreadful affliction, although there was of course a great deal that could be done to help the man. Rick stood up, walked around the desk and put a hand on Whiplash's shoulder to comfort him. To his surprise, a huge hairy hand took Rick's in his own and squeezed it tenderly. Rick felt strangely uncomfortable. Then the man's dramatic blubbing ceased rather too quickly. A sense of unease shot through Rick's mind. He tried to remove his hand from his patient's shoulder, but Whiplash's grip got stronger and he looked up through watery eyes longingly into Rick's face.

"Oh Doctor, you know why it is not working with my wife. I'm queer and I need help. Oh Dr Donovan, ever since I first saw you, I knew you could help me. You see I, I fancy you Rick Donovan." Rick Donovan was panic-stricken. He pulled away his hand from the grasp of the bigger man with all his might and struggled in the direction of the door. But Whiplash was not to be denied and gave chase. He dived for the young doctor's leg and managed to hold onto an ankle.

"Doc, don't fight it. You know you want me. It's all right. It'll be all right," Whiplash squealed.

For Rick Donovan it was far from all right. In fact the whole bloody consultation had turned into a monstrous nightmare of disproportionate dimensions. "Mr Whiplash, I'm afraid it is far from all right, and

I'm afraid your rather strong feelings towards me are most definitely not reciprocated. Now kindly release my ankle or else I'll call security," Rick spoke firmly with as much authority as he could muster.

Whiplash, sensing that the desired reciprocation was not to be, released Rick's ankle then stood up and dusted himself off. The door of the consulting room was opened and two hefty security guards came into the room, the nursing staff God Bless them, realising that all was not well had called Security.

"Everything OK Dr Donovan?" one of the burley guards enquired.

"Yes, thank you. But please could you see Mr Whiplash off the premises." Rick was mightily relieved to see the back of the extraordinary fellow and as he was led away, Rick winced to hear Whiplash whimper, "I really loved him, the bitch," just loud enough so that the clinic nurses could hear.

As soon as Whiplash had been carted off by security and was out of earshot, howls of laughter echoed from the nurses' room. They evidently found Rick's unfortunate predicament extremely funny. They had apparently all been listening at the door after Mrs Whiplash's abrupt departure and had overhead the entire consultation from there on in.

This was probably just as well since security had been subsequently summoned. Dr Rick Donovan, although somewhat aggrieved initially, soon saw the funny side of it after his colleagues had pepped him up with a strong cup of tea and paracetamol for his tension headache. Despite the trauma of the first consultation, a waiting room full of couples remained to be seen and Rick had no option but to dust himself off and continue with the busy clinic. The next couple he saw thankfully appeared to be relatively normal. The female partner had blocked fallopian tubes and Rick put them on the waiting list for IVF. One simple and straightforward consultation at least.

There followed a delightful same sex couple who yearned for their own child, but couldn't quite decide which one of them was to provide the necessary eggs for their future offspring and which one of them was to become pregnant. There was also a minor disagreement about which sperm donor to utilise. Brains like Einstein or muscle like Mr Universe. Eventually, they decided on a nice compromise of a bit of both, a weightlifting astrophysics student from Hull. The three of them joyously laughed at the short-lived indecision and Rick booked their fertility treatment forthwith. The young gynaecologist often pondered at the wonderful diversity and richness of life, and what brilliant parents same sex couples seemed to make. He thought back to Mr Whiplash and felt slightly sorry for the fellow, 'He just needs to find himself Mr Right' Rick murmured to himself.

Then it was the turn of Reverend Williams and his wife. Mrs Williams was a frail little woman of thirty-six years of age who looked as if she was from a bygone era. Her immaculate, white, starched blouse was buttoned up so that not an ounce of flesh was revealed, in keeping with the long, flowing dress that covered her ankles. Her hair was fashioned into a bun that sat primly on top of her head and although she was of slight build, her eyes and demeanour betrayed a fierce and determined temperament. 'Not one to be trifled with,' Rick thought as he introduced himself and bade the couple to sit down. Mrs Williams's handshake was surprisingly as firm as any man's and her manner forthright and business-like. The Reverend Williams, on the other hand, was almost the complete antithesis of his straight-laced wife, both in looks and character. He was a large, rotund, jolly-faced man with a red complexion and laughter lines that echoed his temperament. As he walked in he gave Rick a huge smile, waited for his wife to be seated then sat down himself. Rick took a full history and it so happened that the clergyman and his wife had been trying to conceive for the last three years to no avail. As a couple they seemed oddly suited to each other. She was obviously the stricter of the two and the strong disciplinarian both in terms of religious zeal and daily living. He provided the fun and the lighter side of the relationship and together they seemed to complement each other and make quite a team. When he had finished taking a history, Rick explained the investigations that needed to be carried out. He handed Mrs Williams a number of completed forms for having her blood taken at various times of the month to determine the normality of her cyclical hormone profile. Then to the Reverend Williams he gave a form and a clear plastic pot. Mrs Williams looked quizzically at the pot and then grabbed the form from her husband and started to read the instructions on the back. Her face became contorted the more that she read:

1. The couple should abstain from sexual intercourse for 3 days prior to producing the sample.

2. The sample should be produced by masturbation, aiming directly into the pot.

3. A condom should not be utilised for collection.

4. The withdrawal method should not be utilised for

collection.

5. Please clean your genitalia in the manner shown before producing a sample.

6. Please ensure the sample is delivered to the nurses at the front desk within 1 hour of ejaculation.

"Doctor, is this test really absolutely necessary?" a rather shocked Mrs Williams enquired.

"I'm afraid it is, Mrs Williams. You see, the quantity and quality of your husband's sperm needs to be assessed to ensure it is normal before doing any further more invasive tests on yourself."

"I see. And tell me Doctor what exactly is 'the withdrawal method'?"

The Reverend Williams nearly spat out his dentures. His eyes pleaded with Rick to avoid any explanation of how one pulled out one's old boy just at the last minute. Rick, realising that the Reverend's rather austere wife could only accept a certain amount of sexual revelation at any one time, skilfully avoided a direct answer.

"Well Mrs Williams, it is a medical term used that requires a prolonged explanation and really is not applicable to you and the Reverend here, so please just ignore it."

Mrs Williams seemed only too pleased to disregard the written statement and her husband nodded his gratitude to Rick.

"Doctor, do you think it would possible to give the specimen today, perhaps even this afternoon? It's just that we live some distance from the hospital and I think my wife and I would feel happier getting the test over with at the earliest opportunity." The Reverend coyly requested.

"Ernest, please don't be so disgusting. Just where are you going to produce this um, sample?" Mrs Williams frowned at her husband.

Rick came to the Reverend's rescue. "Well actually, we do have a 'men's room' here in the unit, and as long as you've abstained over the last three days I don't see any reason why you couldn't provide a sample now."

The reverend looked at his wife enquiringly as if to obtain her permission for the deed to be done. Certainly if it had not been for Mrs Williams's strong desire to be a mother, the whole business would have been rejected forthwith. The woman grudgingly agreed and when Rick had completed the consultation he left the office to see if the men's room was free. A fellow had just exited and proudly held a pot in his right hand, which he was presenting to the clinic nurse. Rick looked again and saw the man in question had his left hand and arm in plaster, which was bandaged up in a sling held tightly to his chest. Rick looked down at the pot again. There was definitely something in it.

'How the blazes did he manage to produce it and catch it with just one hand?' he thought to himself, and then dismissed any further thoughts as to how the feat could have been accomplished. After checking that there was no-one else waiting to use the room, Rick ushered the Reverend Williams in. Then turning to the reverend's wife he said, "Mrs Williams, sometimes it helps if the man's partner goes in as well, you know to… um… help."

As soon as he had said it, Rick wished he had not. Mrs Williams gave him a thunderous look and her silence stung like the tip of a whip on bare flesh. She took a seat on the opposite side of the corridor to the entrance of the men's room where she could observe any activity in and out of the room without being in any way associated with it. The Reverend was taken into the room with his instruction pack and left to provide a sample. Rick in the meantime said his goodbyes and returned to his office. He had arranged to see the Reverend and Mrs Williams again in six weeks' time with the results of the various investigations. The next two clinic patients were reasonably straightforward and Rick finally started to relax.

However, later that morning between patients, there was a knock at the door. It was the clinic Sister. "Dr Donovan, a word please."

"Certainly Sister, what can I do for you?"

Sister Humphries, a portly, middle-aged woman, shut the door behind her and spoke in a hushed voice. "Rick, it's the Reverend Williams." Rick raised his eyebrows and looked quizzically at his nursing colleague. Sister Humphries continued. "It's just that he has not come out of the men's room yet."

"Bloody hell! He's been in there for forty-five minutes, what do mean he hasn't come out yet?" Rick got up from his desk and walked towards the exit. "I don't suppose anyone has knocked on the door to find out what the blazes is going on?"

"Well Rick I was, err… we were wondering if you could take a look."

"Oh thanks a billion Sister, another duty for the medic, the saving of distressed wankers!"

Rick strolled out of the office and headed towards where the Reverend Williams was evidently giving his all, presumably without much luck. Mrs Williams saw Rick coming and quickly averted her eyes. Rick, seeing her embarrassment, made no effort to greet her but continued up to the men's room door. He knocked boldly three times and waited. There was a scuffle of activity from within, then the door slowly opened. The Reverend Williams looked ghastly. He was visibly out of breath, looked white as a ghost and beads of perspiration rolled down his forehead. His demeanour was one of defeat as he held up an empty specimen pot. "Poor bastard," Rick thought as he ushered the clergyman back into the room.

"No, no Dr Donovan, please. I just can't do it," the Reverend pleaded with Rick.

"Oh, of course you can Reverend, would it help if I asked Mrs Williams to come in?"

"Oh Lord no, that'll only make matters worse."

"Mmmm… I see. I know what." Rick opened the top drawer of a small cupboard standing within the room. The Reverend gulped. Rick lifted out a collection of girlie magazines that were utilised for such emergencies. A buxom wench clad in only a G-string smiled invitingly at the sweating vicar.

"I can't look at those!" Reverend Williams protested, his eyes wide with amazement. "Mrs Williams would never allow it."

"Well I'm not going to tell her - are you? These investigations really are absolutely necessary Reverend," Rick eased the clergyman's conscience.

"Well, I suppose you are right, Dr Donovan. Perhaps I could try just once more." And with that the Reverend Williams showed Rick to the door. Another half an hour elapsed and still there was no sign of progress and Rick was again called to investigate. Fortunately Bonking Bertha smiling tantalisingly from the middle page had worked her magic for the sweaty vicar. After a gentle knock at the door of the "Men's Room", a beaming Reverend Williams emerged and stood triumphantly with a full pot of semen in his right hand.

"Any problems?" Rick inquired.

"Certainly not. Your medicine did the trick Dr Donovan. I'm sorry it's taken a little while but I did want to fill the pot."

"But Reverend, we only needed a single sample," Rick replied.

"Now Doctor, don't be ungrateful." With that the Reverend Williams called his wife, winked at a rather shocked Sister Humphries, and departed from the clinic, whistling as he went.

CHAPTER 14

The morning fertility clinic stretched well into the afternoon and when it was finally done, Rick headed back to the gynaecology ward to ensure there were no problems to sort out prior to him going home. The Coronary Care Unit just happened to be on the way and as Rick passed it, he felt pangs of guilt. He hadn't enquired about or visited Sir John Rawarse since the day his boss had been admitted. The old man had been pretty decent to Rick, especially in view of the fact that he had paid his bail money. Various sources had reported to Rick that far from being critical of his senior registrar on the night when Belinda Jones had been taken ill, Rawarse had, in fact, been full of praise. Rick stopped in the corridor, turned around and headed toward the main desk of Coronary Care. He looked at the name board of patients on the ward and among nine other names, there was his boss's. Plain old 'John Rawarse' was written on the ward plan as if he was any other old punter who had come off the street with a heart attack. Rick felt a sense of remorse, almost as if a once great man had been reduced to a statistic, another hospital number, and he swore to himself to always treat his patients as individuals. He approached Sir John's bed and found the old man asleep, his breathing was a little laboured and he looked pale and ill. A cardiac monitor flickered silently above his bed and Rick sat down in an adjacent chair. A nurse came by and asked Rick if he was a relative.

"No I'm afraid I'm not. He is my…" Rick was about to say 'boss', then he thought again. He hadn't come to visit the old codger just because he was his boss. Oddly enough Rick had come to realise that Sir John Rawarse was not only a fine clinician and surgeon, but was a cantankerous old bastard with his staff because he wanted the best for his patients. Rick looked at the nurse and finished the sentence. "I'm just a friend." Rick sat with the old man for another twenty minutes or so before Sir John finally opened his eyes.

"Ahh, Donovan, good of you to come." There was a softer, more amenable tone to the old man's voice. In fact he almost sounded pleased to see his senior registrar and before Rick could ask him how he was, he was bombarded with a string of questions.

"How is that young woman you sorted out the other night? You know the one with the ectopic pregnancy who very nearly died. I hear you had a hell of a to-do, even ended up in the damn Police cell. How do you like that, a doctor saves a life, then gets branded a bloody criminal." Sir John coughed, a deep and resounding cough that made the whole of his body shake. Having recovered from the bout he summoned up all his strength and bellowed, "Nurse! Where's my spittoon!" The same staff nurse, looking a little nervous now, hurried to where Sir John lay and handed him a collection pot into which he duly spat. Some rather offensive chewy green phlegm landed in the bottom of the container with a bit of a thud.

When Rawarse had sufficiently recovered Rick responded, glancing down at his boss's medication chart as he did so, "Belinda - err, Miss Jones - is doing very well thank you, sir. In fact, in another two or three days I expect we'll be able to send her home." Rick noted that the old man was not on any antibiotics. If that cough was anything to go by he had a nasty chest infection at best, and pneumonia at worst. "Sir John, forgive for asking but how long have you had that cough?"

"What the hell, trying to be my physician as well now, Donovan, hey?" the old man grumpily remarked. "Well I suppose a day or two. I thought I was getting better until then, but now I have to tell you, I feel bloody sick."

"Do you mind if I just listen to your chest, sir?" Rick picked up a stethoscope as if it were a forgone conclusion.

"Well, um, no I don't suppose I do." As soon as he put the stethoscope on the old man's chest wall Rick knew he had pneumonia. The crackles and wheezes in both lungs indicated a bilateral infection and it made sense that after Sir John had started to make a good recovery this would be the thing to bring him down again.

Rick looked around for the staff nurse who was looking after Sir John and called her over, "Excuse me staff, could you do Sir John's temperature for me please."

The staff nurse looked suitably hostile. "Sorry, just who are you?" she asked in an accusatory fashion.

"Oh, I beg your pardon. My name is Dr Rick Donovan, I'm a friend of Sir John's as well being one of the senior registrars working in this hospital. So if I could trouble you, please."

"Oh sorry, Doctor, but are you this gentleman's doctor?" the nurse was now being obstructive.

Sir John, although obviously weak and tired, had decided that this was enough. "Are you deaf as well as stupid? Just get a bloody thermometer, do you hear me?"

The aggressive ploy seemed to work and the aggrieved nurse sulkily retreated to fetch an electronic thermometer. Rick took it from her and placed it just inside the old man's ear. After a few seconds the gadget beeped, Rick withdrew it and read the scale: thirty-nine degrees. Sir John Rawarse had rampant temperature, reinforcing the diagnosis of pneumonia. Such a complication could certainly compromise his already precarious position. Rick decided to take over; he wrote up some intravenous broad-spectrum antibiotics, ordered a physiotherapist for that evening, and sent off the newly produced sample of phlegm for microbiological assessment. Thereafter he summoned the houseman looking after his boss and after suitable chastisement asked him to carry out arterial blood gas analysis, blood cultures, and a chest X-ray. The staff nurse, realising that an almighty cockup had been made, suddenly became extremely helpful, and when Rick asked for oxygen to be administered and for observations to be carried out every two to four hours, she readily agreed. Finally Rick went back over to Sir John's bed and almost unthinkingly placed a hand on his arm. "We'll get you back hollering at us in no time at all, boss." For the first time ever, Rick experienced the warmth of a sincere smile on Sir John Rawarse's lips.

"I'll visit you tomorrow, you know, to make sure that you're getting better."

"You'd bloody better!" Sir John retorted. Then he closed his exhausted eyes and fell into an unhealthy sleep.

Rick was finally now able to make his way, guilt free, back to the gynaecology ward to check that all was well with his patients. The sister in charge asked him about one patient's medication, and another query about a poor lady who was constipated for which he wrote up the appropriate purgative, but otherwise there was really little else to sort out. So before going home Rick decided to check on Miss Jones. He realised rather ashamedly that it was more for his benefit than for hers, but none the less he strode up to her side room and knocked on the door.

There was a gentle, "Hello, come in," from inside and Rick went in. Belinda looked even lovelier than she had done during their previous meeting and the smile that greeted him warmed him to the depths of his being.

"Hi, I just thought I'd check on you before going home. Is everything all right?"

"Yes, thank you very much Dr Donovan, I'm feeling better and better. It is very kind of you to come and see me again."

Rick felt slightly awkward when the word 'again' was mentioned. Was it so very obvious that he was attracted to this woman? He instantly became more formal and defensive. "Um, very good, I'm pleased you seem to be doing very well... um... clinically." Rick picked up the temperature chart at the bottom of the bed and inspected it. "All your observations seem to be OK, excellent. Well um, have a good evening and I'll see you tomorrow on my ward round."

Belinda seemed hurt by his sudden formality. "Do you have to go just yet?" she softly enquired. Her tone was pleading as if she really didn't want Rick to go. "I know you are very busy but please, there are just a few questions I should like to ask you, if that's OK?" She rolled her beautiful, big green eyes at him and smiled.

Rick could no more refuse this woman than fly to

the moon. He relaxed, returned her smile and sat down on the edge of the bed, waiting attentively for the forthcoming questions. Seconds passed and it was Belinda's turn to appear awkward as she tried desperately to think of some sort of clinical question, anything at all to start the conversation. But her brain and thought processes deserted her in her time of need. It became increasingly obvious that she didn't have anything at all of a medical nature to ask. She started to blush, a magnificent rouge coloured flow that gradually filled her cheeks and was accompanied by a modest lowering of her splendid eyes.

Rick then sensing that she just wanted to be with him, felt his heart miss a beat. He rescued her from her embarrassment. "Perhaps you were wondering how long it would be before you could go home?"

"Oh yes, I was wondering," Belinda quickly responded.

"Well it is likely that you will be OK for discharge in a day or two as long as you continue with your current progress. Is there anyone at home with you?" It was a legitimate question as she had been very ill but Rick was also trying to determine whether or not there was anyone special in Belinda's life.

"No not really, I live by myself, well apart from

177

Charlie of course." Rick groaned internally. He felt the deep down dismay usually associated with the bereavement of a loved one. If this angel was already involved with someone else, what chance was there for him, would they put up a fight for her? He then chastised himself for being so bloody ridiculous. For God's sake he knew nothing about her and so what if she already had a partner called Charlie, although there had been no visitors to speak of that Rick knew about. He was pretty sure that if she had been *his* girlfriend, he would have literally been camping here.

Rick's mind worked overtime. He sighed inwardly and tried to quell his ludicrous feelings. It was probably a temporary infatuation that would blow over in a matter of days, after all it had been a traumatic time recently for both of them, and Rick was not quite sure if he was behaving normally. Then he looked at her again... he felt waves of desire, of wanting to be with her, of wanting to protect her, even having children with her, and growing old with her. So who the hell was Charlie? How close was she to him? Was the bastard good looking? Was the sod rich? And while all this was going through Rick Donovan's mind, the only words he could manage were, "And have you known this Charlie for long?"

"Oh, about a year. My aunt introduced us. Well,

she spontaneously bought him around to the apartment on my last birthday. He is rather cute," Belinda smiled.

"Oh... sorry, did you say it was your aunt who introduced you?"

"Yes, that's right she thought I needed some company on those long winter nights."

Rick's mind was a whirr. What the hell was this girl talking about? He forced a smile then hesitantly asked in something of a subdued voice, "Are you close to this Charlie fellow?"

Belinda was delighted in sensing his jealousy and laughed as long and as hard as her still-sore abdomen would allow her. Rick became slightly annoyed to be the butt of some sort of joke, but she didn't let him fester for too long.

"I suppose I am reasonably close to Charlie. We share a lot of secrets and he is good company, but not too chatty considering he is a goldfish." She beamed an endearing smile directly at him for she knew now that the attraction between them was mutual. Rick perceived what she was thinking and their eyes met again. An unspoken understanding, a meeting of two kindred spirits took place and then Belinda Jones and Rick Donovan started to talk, really communicate.

Initially, it was small talk that gradually progressed into matters that really meant something. The two of them became more and more confident of each other and then shared different aspects of their lives hitherto unspoken. Belinda revealed to him the story of her early life. This included the trauma of the death of her parents in a car crash, and how she was subsequently looked after by her ageing aunt, the same one who had bought Charlie for her. She also confided in him the traumatic events leading up to her emergency admission to hospital, including her meeting and subsequent betrayal by that cad Rupert Daventry.

Rick listened with interest and understanding, with not a hint of judgement but only concern for her wellbeing. It was then Rick's turn to share different aspects of his early life. He was necessarily slightly more guarded when it came to very personal matters since he was still her doctor. His professionalism prevented him from revealing too much and there was certainly never any breach of patient confidentiality. Belinda understood his predicament but did not mind. She trusted him entirely. He had, after all, saved her life.

An hour passed and the couple became oblivious to the passage of time, until a ward nurse knocked on the door and entered the side room. She looked slightly surprised and startled to see Rick. "Oh, I beg your pardon," the nurse fumbled. "Belinda, it's time for your medication."

"It really is about time I went." Rick stood up to go, giving his patient one last smile.

"Thank you so very much, Dr Donovan, for explaining that all so well to me. Perhaps I'll see you tomorrow?"

"Yes of course. I'll pop in to ensure your continued good progress tomorrow morning. Goodnight Miss Jones." With that Rick turned and walked out of the room. It was all he could do to stop himself leaning over and kissing her or least touching her hand to say goodbye. He walked down the ward corridor with a jump in his step. His heart missed a beat and an uncanny knowing descended upon him and lifted his spirits. Never in his life had he talked to a woman the way he had just talked to Belinda Jones. Never had he felt so at home, so at ease in another person's company. It was true that Rick had shagged a fair few women in his life, but he had never felt like this. God, life had some pretty unexpected twists and turns.

CHAPTER 15

Relieved to finally get home, Rick turned the key to open his front door and noticed Enid peering out from her net curtains. Her eyes were fierce and unforgiving. He tried to smile, but it was greeted with a look of contempt so he turned away, and almost sadly, went inside. The telephone rang as he put down his brief case in the hall.

"Hello, Rick Donovan," he murmured absentmindedly.

"Bloody 'ell Rick, you sound a bit depressed. Look, it's Horace here, you know that pain in the bum ambulance driver who's got a nasty habit of phoning you at two in the morning."

"Ah, Horace you old bastard you. How are you doing?" Rick perked up on hearing his colleague's broad accent.

"Well probably better than you. I can't believe you

got nicked for borrowing that old *Mini* so that you could motor up to the hospital to sort out that poor girl. I tell you what, the world 'as gone bloody barmy. Anyhow, Paddy and I were really grateful to you for that night and wanted to take you out for a beer as a way of saying thanks."

"Horace that's really very nice of you both, but I feel a bit tired tonight and…"

Horace cut him short. "No buts or excuses Donovan, we'll pick you up at eight, OK?"

The telephone went dead. There was no point in arguing when there was no one on the other end of the phone. "Sodding paramedics," Rick thought to himself, and then smiled fondly as he thought of Paddy and Horace. "Couldn't hope to meet two more down-to-earth, honest ruffians," he mused, then went upstairs to shower and get ready. When he got out of the shower he remembered that Rachel had said she would ring him, so he checked the answer phone. There were no messages. He sighed, went to the refrigerator, and took out an ice-cold bottle of beer and collapsed on the couch. Then he switched on the box to catch the last ten minutes of Coronation Street.

Rick had just started to doze off when the front door bell sounded. He looked at his watch, ten minutes past eight. As he opened the front door he was greeted by Horace's beaming smile that was always somewhat disconcerting since it revealed the huge gaps in his crooked front teeth.

"Donovan, hurry up man and get your coat, Paddy is holding the taxi."

"OK, Horace, let me just turn the telly off." Having turned the box off, Rick grabbed his coat from the banister in the hall and followed his friend down the short path. Horace had turned around at the gate and was grinning inanely at something. Rick turned around and to his dismay saw Enid at the window, clutching Molly under one arm, and glaring out with a face of disgust.

"Watcha missus, are you all right my old darling?" Horace amicably shouted whilst raising a hand to wave at her.

Enid responded with the frostiest, most disdainful look Rick had so far witnessed to her dentally challenged verbal assailant.

"Bloody 'ell you're a bit ferocious, my old lover," Horace responded, and Rick, fearing another confrontation, bundled his friend into the taxi. To Enid, Horace must have looked like a thug. Certainly the state of his dentition and crew cut, together with his heavily tattooed arms, nicely rounded off with a neat earring, would do nothing to endear him to her. When Horace blew the old girl a kiss from inside the taxi, Rick shuddered at the metaphorical death by contemptuous look on his neighbour's face. "Oh God, I really am going to have to move," he murmured under his breath.

Paddy, who was sitting in the front seat, turned around to greet him. "Donovan, me old mucker, how are you doing?"

"Pad, good to see you, I'm all right you know. How about you mate?"

"Fine Rick, real good." There was a moment's pause before he continued. "That old girl looked a bit pissed off. Is she OK? God, if looks could kill we would have all be shafted with a red-hot poker. That isn't the old bird whose car you nicked to get up to the hospital is it?"

"You got it. My very own neighbour from hell."

"Too risky by half," Horace interrupted, "anyhow, let's talk about more pleasant things for a while shall we? Rick, we thought we'd treat you to a curry with a couple beers chucked in at the Indian on Rosamond Street, followed by a few more bevvies in that new wine bar that's just opened up in town. Good food, good beer, and a bit of skirt, eh? What do you reckon?"

"After the week I've had, it sounds bloody wonderful." Rick replied. "This is really good of you guys to take me out like this."

"Na mate. It was bloody good of you to come to our rescue the other night. I tell you I thought that young lady was on her way to the big sleep. It would have been a real shame too, she was stunner," Paddy added.

Rick's thoughts immediately returned to Belinda and he felt his heart skip a beat. "Yes she is rather lovely," he responded dreamily.

Horace, who had observed the yearning in Rick's facial expression, couldn't help himself. "Hey Pad, look at that. Donovan's looking all lovesick about the girl. You bloody fancy her you old bugger!"

"Oh lads, she is an absolute angel. I've never met anyone like her in my life. Trouble is, she's my patient."

"So, chill out until she's out of hospital and then give her a bell. There ain't anything unethical about that."

"No, I suppose not," Rick replied.

"What about Rachel though? From what I'd heard you two are a bit of an item now, or is she just part of the growing Donovan harem?" Paddy laughed.

Rick was saved from responding as the taxi screeched to an abrupt halt. Paddy nearly smacked his head on the dashboard and on recovering, turned to the fellow driving. "Bloody hell, who the hell do you think you are? Stirling sodding Moss? That is how accidents occur you stupid prat."

The taxi driver thought briefly about telling his passenger to go and f**k himself, but was deterred by Paddy's rather menacing red face and his larger than average frame. Paddy, sensing an obscene retort, raised a spade-like hand menacingly rolled into an enormous fist in full view of the reckless driver.

"Whatever it is you're thinking mate, I'd keep it to yourself unless you want that steering wheel wrapped around your head", Paddy relaxed his fist, "In future just drive a little more carefully, OK?"

The taxi driver nodded that he understood perfectly well and please would his rather ferocious passengers disembark. As they exited, Rick waited for the deluge of abusive obscenities, but none came. Perhaps Paddy's intimidating stare was convincing enough. To his further surprise, after Paddy had paid the fare, the taxi pulled away like a geriatric snail on tranquillisers.

"Gentlemen, I give you a reformed and now model taxi driver." Paddy gave a little bow and walked into the Indian restaurant. Rick looked at Horace in humorous disbelief and the two of them followed their friend inside.

The three colleagues ordered three pints of lager, then painstakingly deliberated over the menu, debating the strength of various curries and the pros and cons of chicken versus lamb. Before they were finally ready to order, the servile and over-gracious waiter had brought them over another pint each. The booze was duly guzzled and Rick's mood started to lighten. The laughter started to flow and their merriment was infectious, spreading to the surrounding tables. Horace and Paddy ordered the lamb and chicken vindaloo on account of the fact that they would be forced to drink more water. In fact it was so hot that three more pints of lager were ordered and sunk with alarming rapidity. Rick remained reasonably conventional and stayed with the mild chicken korma, but found himself matching his colleagues in the drinking stakes pint for pint. Prior to the main course they got through shami kebabs, onion bhajees, samosas, and plates full of poppadums relished with thick gooey chutney. They had all started to really relax.

Over another pint, Rick told his friends about the traumas of his day, ensuring anonymity and excluding medical details, he spoke in particular about his unfortunate liaison with Mr Whiplash and his luckless wife in the fertility unit. When he told them how he had been in danger of being shafted, literally, Paddy and Horace roared with laughter at Rick's misfortune and then ordered more lager. Over double helpings of banana fritters and ice cream, the conversation adopted a more serious tone and turned to the night of Belinda Jones's admission. Paddy recounted the tale of how they found her in her own apartment, lying barely conscious in a pool of her own blood. He spoke of the inefficiency of the casualty department who despite being pre-warned about Belinda's arrival, were ill prepared. Horace nodded his agreement from time to time, taking swigs from his drink while Paddy continued. Then Horace interrupted proceedings to tell his account of the slimy, self-important Rupert Harrington-Smythe and how Paddy smacked him in the gob to effectively prevent him killing their charge. Rick gulped on his fritter and then looked with a concerned eye at Paddy. He had heard rumours about the supercilious little bastard and was aware too that his father was the chief executive of the Trust.

"Oh shit Pad, do you know who Harrington-Smythe's father is?"

"Yeah, the little bastard told me before I punched him."

"He did, did he?" responded Rick incredulously.

"That's right Rick, that night in casualty he told me who he was, and who his precious father is. But like I say I didn't give a shit then and I don't give a shit now," Paddy smiled.

"Oh Pad, I hope for your sake the little sod doesn't press charges, 'cos by all that is holy, his old man could cause you some real trouble."

"Rick, will you chill out? Paddy, please tell the man," Horace interrupted, slurping a swig of lager as he did so.

"Alright, alright. Rick for God's sake don't worry about it. The chief exec is a pussy. He has already sent me a letter." Paddy began to shake with laugher. "Apologising for his snotty-nosed son's actions and congratulating me on a job well done."

"I just do not get it. Harrington-Smythe has got a reputation for being a real bastard and protective of his twat of a son," said Rick, almost disbelieving. "So how come you get away with giving his boy a smack in the gob, even if he did deserve it?"

"Put it like this, Harrington-Smythe Senior and us go back a long way. We know some of the old bastard's history and I can tell you it makes interesting reading. Shagging ward sisters in store cupboards - and different ward sisters at that - would be very interesting news for public consumption, don't you think?"

"You mean you blackmailed him!"

"Oh Rick, how could you say that? We merely reminded him of some past indiscretions, nothing more, nothing less," Paddy rationalised. Horace nodded sagely.

"Way of the world, Rick, way of the world." Horace slurred just a little.

"What about the Police? Did the toe rag call the cops about being assaulted?"

"Oh yer, when he finally woke up."

"So what happened?"

"Well, it just so happens that the A&E staff came up trumps." Paddy paused for another slurp. "Harrington-Smythe called the cops and whilst blubbing inanely described how I whacked him in the smacker."

"So why didn't you get banged up for the night like me?" Rick asked.

"Well, like I said, the A&E staff came up trumps and when the cops asked for witnesses, every single one of the staff said that the twat had tripped over his own feet and whacked himself in the gob!" Paddy chuckled to himself, "and then the cops told the little sod to stop blubbing and that they would charge him for false accusations if he persisted!"

"Happy days, there is some justice. So the poor little sod got turned over by the cops, then probably got a bollocking from his Dad! Life is sometimes sweet!" Rick, Horace and Paddy laughed.

The three friends, ever so slightly staggered, out of the restaurant after Horace had paid the bill and left the grinning waiter an enormous tip. This had the effect of widening his grin to almost impossible proportions as he escorted his customers to the door. They tried flagging down a taxi to no avail and so walked into the town centre. The stroll sobered them up and they arrived at the new wine bar, *The Startled Duck*, feeling the better for their brief exercise in the night air. The entrance of the new club was surprisingly quiet and well-ordered considering the time of night and the quantities of alcohol and testosterone in the atmosphere. Rick looked beyond the well-ordered queue and the reason for such orderliness became apparent. The doorman was an enormous, obscenely muscled giant. His skin was as black as anthracite and his hair shaved so that his head gave the impression of a cannon ball. His look was stern and intimidating, his manner business-like and unfriendly. 'Bloody hell, not one to mess with,' Rick thought to himself as they joined the back of the queue. Then something happened to make the gynaecologist's heart miss a beat. To his horror Rick saw Horace amble up to the murderous looking bouncer and punch him lightly on the shoulder.

"Winston, you bastard, how are you doing me old mucker?" Horace smiled amiably, his few crooked teeth gleaming under the entrance light.

"Oh shit, here we go." Rick had almost wet himself and waited now for the inevitable. The bouncer turned menacingly towards his assailant, his massive fists clenched. Horace was a big man but this fellow dwarfed him by comparison. Rick, who was not usually one to swear, let rip under his breath, "Friggin' hell, we're going to die. Sorry Horace but on this occasion I disown you."

Almost in slow motion, the colossal black knuckles headed for Horace's chin and Rick summoned all his courage just to stay where he was, although the urge to run was almost overwhelming. Throughout it all Horace continued to grin inanely. Then an extraordinary thing happened. The doorman seemed to recognise his foe, his fist slowed right down and the gigantic arm, rippling with steel musculature, relaxed. Winston playfully touched the paramedic gently on the cheek with his enormous fist and then, throwing his massive cannon-ball head back, roared with a deep growling laughter. His brilliantly white teeth contrasted with the blackness of his face and made his merriment seem so much more alive.

"Horace you shithead, good to see you man." And the giant grabbed Horace and hugged him. Horace reciprocated. The two men exchanged brief news like long lost friends and to Rick's astonishment they seemed to be genuinely fond of each other.

"How's little Emily getting on?"

"Good man, real good thanks to you my brother. She started proper school last month and is doing fine. Delilah and I are real proud of her."

"That's fantastic news Winston. I always said she was a fighter eh?" The two of them spoke some more before Winston realised he had been chatting for nearly ten minutes. The crowd was beginning to become restless.

"Horace man, damn good to see you but I gotta do some work now. Grab them honky friends of yours and in you go, this one is on the house. Man, you take good care now, you hear me?"

The two shook hands and before they knew it, the three friends were inside *The Startled Duck* and had been given their first drink for free, courtesy of Horace's mate.

CHAPTER 16

The wine bar was heaving with cavorting, hot and sweaty bodies writhing around in time to the heavy beat that pounded throughout the building. Scantily clad girls displayed their dancing skills and bodies in the hope of attracting Mr Right, and opportunistic males brushed themselves against any female they could for a cheap thrill. The queue at the bar was five deep, and grown adults clambered to obtain the best position to attract the attention of the amply bosomed barmaid. Flashing disco lights shone through the smoky atmosphere, and the aroma of sweat, alcohol and cigarettes mingled with the occasional whiff of something illegal to spice up the already heightened levels of anticipation and sexual excitement.

Rick, Paddy and Horace stood in the midst of this throng of squirming humanity supping a pint of lager each and trying in vain to hold a conversation. After half an hour of hand signals and shouting into each other's ears, Rick came to understand the relationship between the giant bouncer on the door and Horace. Apparently a year or so earlier Horace had been called to a particularly nasty road traffic accident in which a little girl had been knocked down and seriously injured as she innocently came running out of the nursery school gates. Horace told how he had found her, lying in a pool of blood on the pavement, having fallen where the drunk driver had hit her, her mother weeping by her side. She had only been semi-conscious at the time but had looked up into his face and said, "Please Mister, please help me, I don't want to go to heaven yet." She had looked so helpless, so vulnerable and so innocent. Horace had been moved to tears and been made even more determined that she should live. Like so many other road traffic accident victims, the rough paramedic had been instrumental in saving her life. Her name was Emily. By the time Horace had got her to hospital she was unconscious. Emily had then required surgery for a blood clot in her battered brain, and she had teetered on a fine dividing line between life and death before somehow miraculously pulling through. Horace had visited her every day for the month during which she was in hospital, sitting with her, even reading to her, willing her to back to good health. Even after a busy shift he would drop in on the Paediatric Intensive Care Unit to spend some time with her. It was then that he had got to know Winston and Delilah, and had become almost a part of their family.

Such a story warmed Rick's heart but seemed so out of place in the thick swarthy, hedonistic atmosphere of *The Startled Duck*. They all had another drink. Paddy caught the eye of a heavily made-up wench and took her jiving onto the overcrowded dance floor before exchanging oral microbes with an amazingly prolonged snog. Rick and Horace laughed and grimaced as they timed their colleague having a continuous tongue-twirling session of up to three minutes before coming up for air.

A young and very pretty woman with legs up to her armpits and a figure to die for pranced up to Rick and asked him to dance. He declined graciously, his thoughts were with Belinda, and he was pleased that he did so, since not long afterwards her jealous boyfriend proceeded to cause an almighty fracas when he punched the poor bastard who had obviously said 'yes'. All and everyone in the immediate surroundings were astonished at the speed at which Winston sorted out the transgressors of night club etiquette, and they shuddered at the punishment he dished out. The enforced and rapid resolution of the conflict was certainly food for thought for anyone who even thought about starting a fight in *The Startled Duck*. They would clearly need to be drunk as a skunk or a half-wit.

The copious quantities of consumed beer had overfilled Rick's bladder. He left Horace holding his pint and made his way to the lavatory, which was at the far end of the club beyond the bar. On his way, he passed a number of couples groping at each other and frantically snogging in the darkened recesses of the room. He ignored them wondering why they didn't prefer to save such intimacies for the privacy of a hotel room. Just before he reached the toilet, Rick caught a glimpse of someone familiar out of the corner of his eye. It was the red hair he recognised. He looked again. She had her back to him but he knew the contours of those buttocks and shapely legs anywhere. He recognised the way she threw back her magnificent mane of hair as she laughed. Rachel was half sitting, half standing, as her legs straddled the lap of a stranger as he sat on a high bar-stool adjacent to one of the small tables that were scattered throughout the club. Her long, slim arms were drooped around the fellow's neck and she was looking at him intently, seductively, her mouth half-open, inviting him. As Rick watched, the stranger obliged and delved into the warm, moist flesh of her mouth. She responded by pressing herself against his groin. Rick continued to observe with a strange mixture of feelings. On the one hand he felt hurt and betrayed by her disloyalty, on the other, he felt almost relief. Since meeting Belinda Jones he had simply lost interest in any other women. In fact over the last day or two, Rick had felt a strange guilt about neglecting Rachel Smithers, but now as he watched her cavorting with this strange man, any feelings of culpability had all but disappeared.

Rick passed the necking couple as inconspicuously as was possible, he had half a mind to interrupt their smooching but decided to let things just be. As he walked by, Rachel caught sight of him out of the corner of her eye and panicked. She then proceeded, rather too abruptly, to break off from snogging the stranger. The poor fellow looked ever so slightly taken aback and just a bit pissed off following the enforced and rather violent detachment of his slurping tongue, but then to be pushed backwards off his stool for no apparent reason was enough to complete his total disillusionment to his current predicament. He landed with a thud on his backside into a puddle of spilt beer and was clearly not amused.

Rachel for her part didn't know where to look or indeed what to say, to whom. Looking first at Rick she mouthed "Oh God...Rick...I....I am so sorry..." then turning to look at the spurned fellow, with by now, beer soaked trousers, sitting unceremoniously on the wet floor, she yelled, "I am so sorry, I...."

Rick didn't stop but continued past his by-now ex-lover and her rather angry new acquaintance. "I think I'll leave them to it", he thought to himself and then even managed a chuckle, muttering to himself, "Serves you right," and then continued, "anyhow, I've probably done you a favour Rachel, that geezer looked a bit risky."

Rick strolled into the *Gents*, ambled up to the urinal, undid his fly and sighed with blessed relief as he emptied his bladder. The toilets were so arranged that individual urinals were positioned on the far wall and perched above them along the entire length was an enormous vanity mirror, presumably fitted to enable the vain male species to preen himself whilst peeing. Rick took full advantage, admiring himself as he went about his ablutions. The entrance to the toilets was clearly visible in the mirror and Rick intermittently glanced up as a number of other men came in and out of the loos. He ignored them until one particular man walked through the door and headed toward the urinal adjacent to his. Rick's heart sank. He looked again to ensure the identity of the fellow. There was no mistaking it. Mr Whiplash was making his way or rather staggering towards Rick and to make matters worse they appeared to be alone. This was Rick's worse nightmare, to be alone in a public lavatory late at night, with a man who wanted his body. Rick looked down and saw his exposed member protruding from his trousers. Whiplash was half way across the room. A number of horrible thoughts went through Rick's mind and he frantically struggled to replace his willy back into the safety of his underpants. In his frenzied attempts he caught his old boy halfway along its length in the stainless steel zip of his trousers. He screamed in agony as the metal chewed into his old boy and Whiplash, who had up until that point been oblivious to Rick's presence, looked up inquisitively. Rick bowed his head so as not to reveal his identity in the mirror and shuffled sideways towards an empty cubicle, gritting his teeth and trying desperately to undo the zip that gripped his pride and joy.

"Can I help?" Whiplash slurred.

"Umm, no… thank you." Rick tried to disguise his voice by mumbling. He made it to the cubicle and slammed the door closed bolting it as he did so. With

Whiplash out of sight for the moment, he fought to release his dick from its current predicament and after a struggle it finally came free. It was, to say the least, somewhat bruised and battered and Rick gently replaced it within the sanctuary of his trousers. Meanwhile, outside the cubicle enlightenment had come to Whiplash. He had been slightly confused initially as to the strange behaviour of the bloke at the urinal but now recognition dawned. After completing his ablutions he approached the restroom door and opened and closed it to give the impression that he had gone about his business and left. He then tiptoed as quietly as possible so that he stood just outside Rick's cubicle and waited. Rick, in the meantime, listened intently for any signs of life outside the cubicle door. After an acceptable period of time had elapsed he gingerly opened the lock and stepped outside the cubicle. Whiplash pounced, trying to force Rick back into the cubicle for a bit of rumpy-pumpy.

"My lovely boy, you came back to daddy!" he drunkenly shrieked. By this time, Rick was really starting to get a bit pissed off. He pushed the amorous man backwards trying to get past him as he did so, but to no avail. Now desperate, Rick swung a flailing fist in Whiplash's direction and landed a cracker on his nose. Whiplash, although dazed, responded by lunging for Rick's nether regions and the fight was on. Rick head- butted the maniac and drove him backwards towards the restroom door. They spilled out into the nightclub proper and landed on a group of louts whose drinks were subsequently spilt and whose tempers now flared. The fighting spread so that soon the entire corner of the night-club was a mass of flying fists, boots, glasses and chairs. Rick, much to his relief, became separated from Whiplash, but was knocked to the floor by some unknown assailant. With his vision blurred and his head thumping, he was much relieved to feel a pair of strong arms physically lift him back into a standing position and support him as he swayed to and fro.

"Come on me old mucker, time to leave." Horace supported his friend and was soon joined by Paddy. Together they almost carried Rick out from the hordes of fighting men and women. Among the confusion and the panic, Rick heard a scream of someone he recognised. To one side of the room, through the smoky atmosphere he could just make out Rachel. She was being slapped about by the same rough-looking fellow who evidently had designs on her. Rachel's assailant was making the most of the confusion and tore at her clothing in the semi-darkness, groping her and forcing her to the floor.

Rage then filled Rick's being and, shaking off his friends, he determinedly charged through the crowd towards Rachel, closely followed by Horace and Paddy. He pulled Rachel's attacker off her and smacked him straight in the face. Blood poured from the man's mouth and as he looked at Rick, Rick willed him to get up and have a go. But as is often the case with most bullies, he was scared now. He cowered on the floor and looked away from Rick's fuming eyes. Then the gynaecologist helped Rachel up and placed a coat around her shoulders to hide her nakedness beneath the torn clothing. With Paddy and Horace flanking them they forced their way towards the main entrance of *The Startled Duck* and out into the fresh night air. Standing on the pavement outside, Horace had a strange premonition that something terrible was going to happen to Emily's father. He quickly returned inside and looked for Winston. His friend was in the middle of the dance floor, and appeared to be gaining some control over the fighting throng. But as Horace squinted through the dimly lit nightclub, he realised Winston was in dire danger. He charged towards him and caught the man's arm as it swung towards the big black bouncer. The startled stranger dropped the knife and an instant later followed it to the floor as Horace rendered him unconscious with a blow to the temple. Winston swirled around and saw the man lying prone with the knife beside him. He looked at Horace and smiled. Winston immediately understood and nodded gratefully at his friend.

"I owe you one my friend." Winston's teeth gleamed like a Colgate advert.

"No worries. Thanks for the drink. We'll see you soon. Love to Delilah and Emily." And with that Horace left Winston to clear up the remaining stragglers and returned to his friends, who were waiting outside the nightclub.

The four of them walked slowly up the high street towards the taxi rank. Rachel was nestled under Rick's arm and by now she had stopped sobbing. They were a good fifty metres from the club when they heard the police sirens wailing. A big *BMW* panda car screeched to a halt outside *The Startled Duck* and as the doors of the Police car opened, an array of paper food cartons and debris spilled out onto the pavement. Then two rather large police officers stepped out of the car and waddled into the nightclub. Roger and Dave were not having a good night. They hadn't even had time to finish their Big Macs between calls. Further police reinforcements arrived at the scene and before long the place was alive with flashing blue lights. The street soon swarmed with blue uniforms and revellers were being dragged out of the club in handcuffs before being pushed into waiting vans. Rick couldn't help chuckling when he saw Whiplash being dragged out of the night club and handcuffed. It was the second time in a matter of hours that the wretched man had been manhandled away. Roger and Dave were the arresting officers, which seemed to Rick to be quite fitting.

Rick, Rachel, Horace and Paddy all climbed into the same taxi and headed for home. Horace was the first to speak up. "Well come on Rick, what happened? You can't start the mother of all nightclub fights without letting your mates in on why it started it."

"You really want to know eh? Well one sentence sums it up... I'm having a pee... in the Gents... when old Mr Amorous walks in, you know the one I was telling you about in the restaurant!"

"Bloody 'ell, you mean the geezer who tried it on in your clinic this afternoon?"

"The very same. Only this time my old boy is hanging out and I feel decidedly more vulnerable."

"No bloody wonder there was a punch up. Ah well, all's well that ends well," Paddy added. "Well I take it all is well. I mean he didn't manage to get a grip on your todger, did he?" Paddy smirked and Horace damn near wet himself trying to hold back the laughter.

"No, he bloody didn't," Rick replied angrily. Horace couldn't help himself. He started to laugh, great bursts of unadulterated mirth. Paddy joined in at the image of Rick standing in front of the urinal with Whiplash mincing through the door and fancying his chances. The alcohol and the relief of escape fed their zany humour.

The laughter was infectious as always and before long Rick too was chuckling. "By the way, thanks for pulling me out guys. All I needed tonight was to be arrested again by those fat coppers."

"Don't mention it you ol' bastard," responded Horace and Paddy in unison. "It was our pleasure," Paddy slurred. The atmosphere went quiet again and only the quiet revving of the engine between gear changes could be heard.

Then Rachel, having thoroughly dried her eyes, whispered, "Umm, thanks to you as well Rick, for pulling that shit off me. I will admit to being really scared."

Rick smiled and hugged her to him. "No problem

Rachel. You know in a way we were both in the same boat tonight. You get assaulted by some arsehole, as I damn near did too, there's an almighty punch-up and we all get out just in time. It's a great life isn't it?" The two of them looked at each other fondly. They both knew now that their romance was doomed but there was no reason why they could not remain good mates.

"Friends?" Rachel ventured.

"Friends," Rick agreed.

"Well thank God for that!" Horace boomed from the front seat. "Driver, forget the original address. 15 Fanny Street please." Then, turning to his friends, said, "Right you lot we're all going back to my place for a night cap or two, OK?" No one objected and the camaraderie continued into the early hours of the morning.

It was 4 a.m. when Rick tiptoed up to his front door and let himself in. His movements simulated those of a drunken would-be thief skulking up to a house he intended to do over. Despite the clanging of the gate and the milk bottles that were knocked over - the sound of which carried down the entire street - his neighbours remained apparently undisturbed. Silence returned once more to the road. Once inside his terrace house, Rick clambered up the stairs. He just about managed to remove his clothes and then collapsed, exhausted, on the bed. It had been an eventful day, not to mention night. Rick lay there with his eyes half open staring up at the ceiling. His mind buzzed around and around with thoughts of the last twenty-four hours; thoughts of Belinda, thoughts of Sir John Rawarse, both lying in their respective hospital beds. Thoughts of barking patients like Whiplash and how they could so easily ruin a doctor's life. Rick thought of his down-to-earth friends, Horace, Paddy and Rachel. Rachel... she was a good friend, but had turned out to be an unfaithful lover. Her infidelity had freed him from any romantic ties. His mind returned to Belinda Jones and he smiled to himself before falling into a deep and contented sleep.

CHAPTER 17

The following morning was a real struggle. Both the lack of sleep and the effect of alcohol had worn Rick down, yet there was a lightness of his heart that gave him the energy to be up and ready for what the day would throw at him. Having caught the early bus that was on time for once, he arrived at the hospital by 9 a.m. and headed straight for the office. The departmental secretaries were already at their computers, busy typing away, their fingers dancing lightly on the keyboards like concert pianists. Rick greeted them with his best smile and bade them a 'croaky' good morning. He then proceeded to look through the morning mail and sorted the chaff from the wheat, chucking the usual junk mail into the bin. A letter marked 'Private and Confidential' with a post mark from London caught his eye. He folded it in two and placed it in his top pocket for reading later in private.

Rachel popped her head around the door. "Morning boss. Ready for the ward round?" she chirped good-humouredly.

"Err... morning Rachel. Yup, I'll be with you now." There was no awkwardness or embarrassment following the events of the preceding night. All that had been ironed out during the numerous nightcaps at Horace's place. Despite their hangovers, they were both resilient and full of energy. There was work to be done, patients to be attended to and the two of them got on with it like colleagues and friends. The usual round of gynaecological and obstetric problems were encountered and dealt with swiftly and efficiently. The last patient they reviewed was Belinda Jones and as they entered her room, Rick thought how utterly radiant she looked. He wanted to stay and talk to her, to spend more time getting to know her, but professional etiquette precluded such behaviour. She was doing particularly well; her observation charts showed no abnormality and the staff nurse present hinted at the possibility of her going home.

"Well, Belinda you look terrific this morning. Are you eating? Drinking? Peeing? Bowels opened yet?" Belinda nodded an affirmative to each of the questions, her big green eyes searching Rick's face and her mouth turning upwards at the edges to form a radiant smile that melted his heart. As much as Rick hated the thought of her no longer being his charge, he knew she was fit to go home and besides which, the cash-strapped NHS needed the bed.

"Now you can't go home to an empty apartment, and Charlie does not count." Rick smiled as he recounted their previous conversation about Belinda's goldfish and the subliminal teasing he wantonly enjoyed. Dr Rachel Smithers just looked perplexed. Rick continued, "You have just had major surgery, is there anyone who can stay with you until you're fully recuperated?" Rick wished he could take her home himself.

"Well, Mr Donovan, I have an aunt who lives locally. I'm sure she wouldn't mind if I stayed with her for a week or so, just until I'm fully fit again."

"Excellent. If that is the case, then I'm happy for you to go this afternoon," Rick said matter-of-factly. In truth he was anything but happy for her to be discharged. When would he see her again? How could he get to know her properly?

"I don't quite know how to thank you and your team, you've all been quite fantastic. I realise I'd be in a wooden box by now without you all. So thank you from the bottom of my heart." Even Rachel was taken aback by this girl's sincerity and returned her smile. The medical staff filed out of the room and Rick was the last to leave. He turned around to catch a glimpse of her. His spirits soared for she put her fingers to her lips and kissed them before blowing the kiss in his direction. It was at least some kind of acknowledgement that she felt the same way as he did. His feelings got the better of him, and disregarding any social or medical protocol, but still ensuring that none of his colleagues were looking, he simulating catching her kiss in his hand which he then placed on his heart. Her face lit up with a look of knowing contentment and it took all of Rick's self-discipline not to go to her and hold her.

"Rick, are you coming to clinic?" Rachel broke the spell.

"Um, yes, I'll just go and see how Sir John is doing."

"OK, I'll come with you if you like. Be interesting to see how the boss is doing." The two of them made their way to the Coronary Care Unit in silence. Sir John was sitting upright in his bed reading The Times as they approached.

"Ah, Donovan my boy, good to see you. You'll be pleased to know that your cantankerous old boss is on the mend thanks to you. These bloody medics can't see beyond the end of their noses." Rawarse looked up at one of the passing cardiology doctors and gave him a contemptuous look. "They can't even diagnose simple pneumonia," he offered in a raised voice and then, chuckling, added, "It takes a gynaecologist to do it for them."

"Good to see you looking better, sir. The antibiotics have obviously kicked in."

"They bloody well have Donovan, and now I owe you for saving my life not once but twice. God, what an outrageous thought. It is the first time in my career I've ever been indebted to one of my juniors." The old man's hardened facial features softened almost into a smile and he added, "Rick, I am not used to this so bear with me", the old man stuttered and then out it came, "I just wanted to say… thank you."

Rachel gasped at the change in Sir John's temperament. However, she reflected that anyone that close to death would be forced into a reflective mood and would evidently feel some gratitude toward any benefactor. She was almost relieved when he turned on her. "You girl, stop looking so gormless. There must be some work to be done, clinics to be sorted. Go and get on with it."

Rick and Rachel turned to leave when Rawarse called after them, "And I am grateful to you *both* for coming to see me." This time he really was smiling at them. It was the first occasion that Rachel had ever witnessed him smile at her.

The morning sun had shone brilliantly through the bedroom window and the bright light had roused Enid from her slumber. Her arm had reached down over the edge of the bed and stroked Molly. It was something she did every morning as much for her own comfort and reassurance, as for Molly's. The morning passed quite quickly and Enid completed most of her chores in reasonably good time. The telephone rang and Enid checked her wig in the mirror before picking up the receiver, almost as if the suspected caller had the ability to see her as well as speak to her.

"Hello, this is 246543. Miss Jones speaking."

"Hello, Aunt Enid, this is Belinda. I'm calling you from the hospital."

"I know where you are calling me from my girl, now how are you?"

"Well that's what I'm calling about. The surgeon saw me this morning and said that he's happy for me to go home as long as I have some company. I was wondering if I could…"

Enid cut her off in mid-flow. "You must come and stay here with me for as long as you like my child. I can't have you going back to the flat all by yourself, not after what you've been through."

"Oh thank you Aunt Enid. That's fabulous. Do you know they have been so kind to me here. The doctor looking after me has been especially wonderful, I'd trust that man with my life you know, but I do really want to get out of hospital now."

Again Enid felt a burst of gratitude towards the medical staff who had saved Belinda's life. "When do you want me to fetch you?"

"Any time this afternoon would be brilliant."

"Excellent my dear. I have a church luncheon with some broken bridges to repair, but I can pick you up around four o'clock. Do you remember my colleague Miss Mavis Guillegiato, you know the one who thinks she is an Italian opera singer?"

"Umm, not really…." Belinda was slightly confused.

"Well anyway, her and my Molly had a bit of a to do at a prayer meeting at my house a few days ago, all a bit silly really ….but I need to sort out some kind of reconciliation you see, a bit of Nelson Mandela type diplomacy and forgiveness...hence the luncheon. In any case forget about that, I'll be there about four o'clock to collect you, Molly and I will see you then."

"That would be great. Thank you Aunt Enid."

"All right my dear, four it is then, goodbye Belinda."

The gynaecology clinic was heaving and overbooked as usual. Rick and his colleagues rushed from patient to patient. Spies from the management were auditing how long patients had to wait, and whether they were satisfied with the setup of the clinic. As far Rick was concerned they could also assess whether he was satisfactorily sweeping the consulting room floors with a broom up his arse. NHS cut backs had meant that ridiculous measures to save pennies had overshadowed the need to provide good patient care. Rick knew it was going to be a difficult afternoon when his first patient walked in with two burly, loutish looking minders, presumably her sons, and demanded satisfaction. Rick carefully explained that he would need to take at least a rudimentary history and perhaps if she didn't mind a cursory examination before deciding on the best management plan for her problem which just happened to be painful periods and excruciating sex.

The good lady having accepted this much, burst into a flood of tears and called Rick a bloody pervert when he asked exactly where the pain was in her pelvis and whether it was worse during her periods or when intimately engaged in a spot of nookie. At this point her two family bodyguards started to become somewhat agitated and Rick found himself apologising, although he was not quite sure what for, and handed her a box of tissues that he kept for such emergencies. The remainder of the consultation was equally uninformative and Rick decided on delaying tactics by ordering a scan and arranging for the unfortunate woman to be seen by a psychiatrist.

The next consultation was equally difficult. As the ill-fated patient waddled into the room, Rick realised that he had never seen such an enormous woman in all his life. She was truly gargantuan. She was so obese that when he tried to examine her, her huge frame overlapped the examination couch on both sides. It took a further twenty minutes to move the examination couch in from the adjoining room and place it adjacent to the existing couch to essentially form a 'double' couch. Only then could Rick do his examination of her bits justice. The assessment left him panting, beads of sweat breaking out on his forehead, his arms aching from the shear strain of holding back rolls of adipose in his attempts to obtain reasonable views of her nether regions. Despite such difficulty Rick completed the necessary examination and obtained her willing agreement on a weight loss programme. He was further chuffed that she seemed determined to help herself and was pleased with his suggested management plan. The gynaecologist pondered that, fat or thin, short or tall, black or white, straight or gay, looney left or nutter right...at the end of the day every patient was a human being, and every patient deserved help and respect. Rick was not entirely sure that this ethos applied to NHS managers since following his difficult series of consultations and examinations, Rick's only reward apart from throbbing limbs was the triumphant look on the auditors' faces now that he was well and truly behind time.

And so the clinic rolled on, sometimes straightforward and sometimes downright difficult. At a quarter to five Rick let out a sigh of relief as the final patient exited the clinic. He reclined back into his chair and could almost have kissed the nurse who brought him in a cup of tea. He dictated letters on each of the patients to their respective GPs, and then feeling in his top pocket pulled out the official-looking post he had received that morning. He opened the letter and scanned down the page, the look of alarm on his face increasing with every line that he read:

The General Medical Council

London

England

Ref: #1 R.Donovan/Guilty Bastard

Dear Mr Donovan

It has recently been brought to our attention by your hospital Trust that you have been involved in behaviour incompatible with your status as a registered medical practitioner. The beating up of old ladies and the stealing of a motor vehicle (Austin Mini) is not generally considered appropriate behaviour for members of the medical profession.

Your actions have certainly brought the profession into disrepute. We believe that the police have been involved and you may have a court case pending. In view of this serious breach of conduct, the matter has been referred to the Fitness to Practice committee. In the meantime we have suggested to your hospital Trust that you are carefully monitored. The issue of suspension from all professional duties will be determined by your hospital executive until this disciplinary matter has been resolved.

Yours sincerely,

G A Snodgrass

The clinic nurse popped her head around the door. "Dr Donovan, there is a telephone call for you in the office. Shall I transfer it through?"

"Yes, thanks if you would. More good news I'm sure." Rick had an inkling of the nature of the call. The phone on the desk rang. Rick picked it up. "Hello, Rick Donovan."

"Ah, Dr Donovan, this is Mr Kurfew here… from medical personnel."

"What do you want? Now let me see - possibly to congratulate me on a good job done whilst there has been no senior cover, possibly to offer me a knighthood for services rendered to the hospital trust? Or did you just fancy a chummy little chat?"

"There really is no need for sarcasm you know. I'm afraid, doctor, that following consultation with the GMC, the Trust has decided to suspend you until your current disciplinary matter has been cleared up once and for all."

"I see. Presumably the flu epidemic is now over, staff are back at work and I'm expendable again. Good of you to ring me at the end of the working day. Let him do the clinic then shaft him with the good news eh?"

Andrew Kurfew ignored Rick's comments and continued. "I've sent all the paperwork regarding your suspension to your home, now if you don't mind I've got better things to do."

"Well thanks for coming to tell me in person, and for breaking the news so nicely. Incidentally, who contacted the GMC?"

"I did, Dr Donovan." There was a triumphant note to Kurfew's tone of voice.

"Well thank you once again you ignorant arsehole and go to hell." Rick put the phone down before Kurfew could respond.

CHAPTER 18

Rick departed from the clinic feeling pretty desolate. Before leaving the hospital he called into the ward to see if Belinda was still there. He knocked on the side room door and after a moment's waiting entered. The room was bare and empty, the bed had been stripped and remade with clean linen ready for the next patient. "Well Belinda, I am at least pleased that you've managed to get home. I just hope you're being well looked after," Rick spoke out loud. "Who knows, maybe our paths will cross again."

As he trudged out of the hospital Rick felt more lonely and depressed than he had for a long time. He walked with an air of defeatism, his shoulders were hunched, his frame slightly stooped and head down as he shuffled out of the main hospital entrance. Even the porters who normally greeted him with a friendly "G'night Doc," seemed to ignore him. He tried rationalising his behaviour on the night he forcibly took Enid's car. In his mind he went over and over whether he could have got to the hospital in time without resorting to such tactics, but time and time again it came back to the same thing. Belinda Jones would have died that night if he hadn't acted illegally. In the eyes of the law he may have done wrong, but morally Rick still felt completely justified. He thought of Belinda's state when he arrived in the operating theatre, she had just survived a cardiac arrest, and he recalled her pallor to be a sickening, almost translucent white. She had looked like a ghost, a corpse. He then remembered her on ICU, holding her hand, willing her to recover and subsequently her radiant smile as she was nursed back to physical health. Rick reflected that it had all been worth it. His career was precious to him, but not as precious as her life and wellbeing or indeed any other person or patient's life for that matter.

The medic stood at the bus stop outside the hospital with horizontal drizzle soaking him right down to his underpants. It really hadn't been a good end to the day. He was pissed off with late buses, pissed off with the hospital, pissed off that he might never see Belinda again, and now to top it all he was getting pissed on. The bus pitched up twenty-five minutes late. It was, appropriately, number 13. The only seat available was right at the back of the vehicle, next to a rather drunk looking fellow with a red nose. Having nearly impaled himself on an outstretched umbrella, that some silly cow had left sticking out into the aisle, Rick managed to reach the spare seat and gratefully sat down. It was only then that he realised why there was no one sitting in it. The drunkard on closer scrutiny appeared to be a youngster and was so pissed that he was bordering on the unconscious. He had kindly shared the contents of the cider bottle with his imaginary friend in the adjacent seat, the one that Rick had now lowered his bum onto. Rainwater and scrumpy mingled to make the dog bites on Rick's arse sting. There was no point in remonstrating with the intoxicated fellow since he was by now snoring his head off in a comatose bliss.

"Bloody buses, bloody youths" Rick muttered under his breath, and then contemplating the delay in his insurance company sorting out the cash for his stolen Mini, which in turn necessitated his use of the *Cardiff Bus Company*, he added "and bloody insurance company."

The bus gently swerved around a corner and the intoxicated youth's head descended onto Rick's shoulder and remained there. The boy nestled closer to Rick and grunted something about "mummy".

Despite the adverse circumstances Rick found himself in, he couldn't help feeling a bit sorry for the kid resting on his shoulder. Rick allowed him to rest his head and did not move, but whispered softly, "I wonder what crap you've had to endure to make you pissed out of your skull at this time in the day. You poor sod."

As a way of reply the youngster promptly threw up into Rick's lap. Rick had never seen so much vomit in all his life. It overflowed off his thighs, dribbling in semi-solid lumps onto Rick's shoes and the floor.

"Oh friggin' hell." Rick couldn't help the expletive as he jumped clear of the next batch of projectile vomit heading in his direction. He looked down at his shirt, trousers and shoes in horror. They were barely recognisable. The smell of partially digested food, combined with copious quantities of cider and stomach secretions, filled Rick's nostrils and made him retch. He shouted futilely, "You silly little bastard!"

Then something even more awful happened. The boy gasped horribly, half inhaled a whoop of air and immediately started to turn blue.

"Oh Shit." Rick knew that he had inhaled a solid piece of vomit and if he didn't act quickly this boy's life would be no longer. "Bollocks, bollocks,

bollocks!" he mouthed as the other passengers on the bus watched him incredulously pick up the boy from the seat, place his arms around his upper abdomen and thrust inwards and upwards on the youth's belly. "Someone call a bloody ambulance!" Rick shouted as he continued his Heimlich manoeuvre and a surly looking character three seats in front pulled out his mobile phone and obliged. Seconds seemed like hours as Rick struggled to rid the boy of the debris blocking his windpipe. Finally, on the fifth Heimlich thrust a piece of food shot out of the boy's mouth and into the path of a well-dressed, rather well-to-do, middle-aged woman with half-moon spectacles balanced on the end of her nose. The woman screamed in horror as the vomit hit her squarely in the face, so that her view of the world was diminished because of her vomit-covered spectacles. All semblance of respectability evaporated as she let rip a stream of obscene language.

By now all the passengers on the bus were watching with morbid fascination as the drama unfolded before their very eyes. Rick in the meantime had laid the lad on the floor of the bus and now felt his pulse. "Still there, thank God," he mumbled to himself. He then put his ear to the boy's mouth to listen for breathing. Nothing! Not a sound and not the faintest movement of the chest wall. Rick wiped away the vomit from the youth's mouth with the sleeve of his coat. He pinched the boy's nose between his thumb and forefinger, and put his lips over the boy's mouth before breathing into his oxygen-starved lungs. The lad coughed and spluttered, spraying Rick with a mixture of gastric contents and phlegm, and then started to breathe again.

The relief on that Cardiff bus was palpable, and Rick despite all his current woes and being covered in puke, smiled then laughed that this young lad had been grabbed back from that bastard, the angel of death. The crowd on the bus whooped, cheered and applauded. Rick tilted the boy over onto his side and into the recovery position. He stood up, brushed any remaining vomit off his by now ruined clothes and smiled at his fellow passengers who continued to applaud.

The bus driver had very sensibly stopped the vehicle and the wail of an ambulance siren could be heard approaching. Before anyone knew it, Paddy and Horace had bounded out of their ambulance and on board the stationary bus. Initially the paramedics didn't notice Rick. They rushed to the boy lying on the deck and checked his pulse and breathing. Horace inserted an airway then applied an oxygen mask whilst

Paddy inserted a drip into the boy's hand to give him some intravenous fluids. Content then that their charge was in no imminent danger, they looked up and around at the vomit-strewn seats and floor. Horace saw the empty bottle of cider lying under the seat. "Daft little bugger. Obviously got pissed as a fart, honked up, then aspirated on his own puke," Horace surmised.

"Excellent, gentlemen. Your clinical appraisal of the scene is correct," Rick surprised them both.

"Bloody 'ell, Donovan what the hell are you doing here?" Paddy responded. "And by God, you look like shit, Rick."

"Vomit, to be precise. I look like vomit. Your patient was as you say, intoxicated, which indeed caused him to vomit copious quantities of lumpy puke all over my best overcoat, shirt, trousers and shoes. After ruining the entirety of my current wardrobe, he aspirated and lucky for him that Mr Heimlich's manoeuvre was effective. You might also note that there appears to be what looks like half-chewed tablets in what he has thrown up. I suspect that he may well have overdosed in addition to his excessive alcohol consumption, poor sod."

"Oh right… um, thanks Rick, when we get him to

A & E, I'll get them to do a toxicology screen and when he wakes up the shrinks will no doubt want a word."

"No doubt. I'll see you boys later." Rick sighed wearily, momentarily closing his eyes as he did so. It had been one hell of a day and now the adrenaline had stopped flowing Rick felt the great weight of his suspension from the hospital and indeed the letter from the *GMC*. Knowing him well, Horace and Paddy picked up that their friend was far from right. They knew he was by now almost at the end of his tether.

Horace especially perceived something beyond this drunken youth was amiss. "Rick, are you OK, mate? You seem a bit edgy. A little bit of vomit doesn't normally affect you."

"Don't worry about me old mate, but thanks for asking anyway." Rick feigned a half-hearted smile.

Horace was not to be denied and persisted. "It's got nothing to do with Belinda Jones case has it?"

Rick remained quiet and Horace knew that something was up. "Something has happened at the hospital." Rick's silence confirmed the big man's suspicions.

"The bastards, they have suspended you again, haven't they?"

"Horace, you are a good friend but it isn't your problem. I think I might get off the bus here. It would appear safer to walk." Rick gathered his briefcase, flicking a piece of vomit off the handle as he did so, and walked down the aisle of the bus to the applause and calls of "Well done! Fantastic! You saved that boy's life! You are a hero!" from the general public on board.

One man stepped out with a sophisticated looking camera and took Rick's photograph. "Sir, I wonder if I might have a few words, I'm from the local press. You just saved that boy's life and…" The photographer stopped in mid-sentence as Rick pushed past him.

"I am very sorry, but all I want is to get home, put my clothes in the dustbin and have a hot bath."

"Could I at least have your name, sir?" But it was too late. Rick was off the bus and striding purposefully homebound. Horace and Paddy had in the meantime busied themselves placing the unfortunate boy, complete with IV lines and oxygen, onto a stretcher and were now carrying him off the public transport towards the ambulance. Horace, who had witnessed the exchange between Rick and the journalist, spoke up as they hauled the stretcher past the newspaper man. "His name is Dr Rick Donovan. He works at the local hospital and is one of the best goddamn doctors they've got. You've just seen him save that boy's life. We've seen him save many lives and guess what? The hospital has just bloody well suspended him for saving the life of a girl that my colleague and I recently got called to."

The reporter's eyes lit up. He sensed a story beyond what he had just witnessed. He followed the paramedics out to the waiting ambulance, taking photographs as he went. "Really?" he said. "And what's your name sir?"

"Just call me Horace, and this is my colleague, Paddy. We've both been working these streets for the past seventeen years as paramedics. We both know what we're talking about and believe you me, Dr Donovan is one of the best." Having secured their charge inside the vehicle, Horace closed the ambulance doors.

"My name's Geoff Woodruff, I work for The Daily News. Would you guys be prepared to give statements? I'll make it worth your while."

Horace handed the journalist a piece of scrap paper with a contact number on. "You tell us where and when. We'll be there." With that Horace and

Paddy climbed into the ambulance and sped off in the direction of the hospital.

CHAPTER 19

A few days had passed since Belinda's discharge from hospital and Enid was up at the crack of sparrows busily tidying up, fussing around and generally pampering her niece. Belinda was awoken with a mug of steaming tea followed by a tray of cereal, eggs, bacon, mushrooms, sausages and toast. Molly trotted into the room behind her mistress, gently holding the morning papers in her mouth.

"Good morning my dear, did you sleep well?" Enid spoke softly as she drew the curtains open and let in the morning sunshine.

"Oh, Aunt Enid, yes thank you." Belinda yawned lazily, squinting her eyes against the daylight. She sat up to face the enormous breakfast that her aunt had placed in front of her. "Golly, cooked breakfast again, anyone would think you're trying to fatten me up."

"You've got to get your strength back dear and I'm here to make sure that you do." Enid smiled kindly at her niece. She had been so worried about Belinda, but now contented herself that her recovery was proceeding at a satisfactory pace. Molly dumped the papers by the side of the bed and was sitting patiently, her greedy little eyes focused on the plate of bacon and sausages. The little dog had put on a considerable amount of weight since Belinda's arrival and was content to carrying on doing so. Belinda in the meantime was happy that the hound was so obliging. She slipped the little mutt a sausage and it was gone in less than a split second.

"It looks like a lovely day, dear. What do you want to do, well besides rest of course? Perhaps we could have a game of Scrabble?" Enid asked. She had thoroughly enjoyed looking after Belinda. It somehow gave her life a bit more of a purpose and quashed the loneliness she felt deep down inside. Molly was great company but not quite the same as another human being.

"Err, yes of course Aunt Enid, if you would like. I was also wondering that since it is such a lovely day, I might perhaps take a gentle stroll to the corner shop and buy a card and a nice bottle of wine for Mr Donovan, you know, as a thank you." The young woman's face lit up at as she spoke his name and her heart thumped faster at the thought of him. It was obvious even to the old lady that Belinda had romantic feelings for the fellow but the pensioner was slightly puzzled.

"Sorry dear, but who is Mr Donovan?"

"Oh, Aunt Enid you know, the surgeon who saved my life." Belinda hadn't stopped talking about the dashing young surgeon who had saved her life, but this was the first time she had mentioned him by name. Enid hadn't really paid much attention since the consultant surgeon's name above Belinda's hospital bed was Sir John Rawarse. Now the name Donovan made the old lady shudder since it was also the surname of her obnoxious next door neighbour. She had established the fact when some of his mail had been put through her letterbox by mistake. A flash of unwelcome insight intruded Enid's conscience. Rick had said he was a doctor on the night he had assaulted her and stolen her car. Although she was not listening at the time, she thought she remembered the police commenting that Rick was a gynaecologist. The old woman's mind raced. Had he stolen the *Mini* on the same night as Belinda was taken into hospital? Her mind was all in whirl.

"Aunt Enid, are you alright? You look a little pale."

"Oh, um, yes child. Did you say Rick Donovan?"

"Golly Aunt Enid, how did you know his first name was Rick?" Enid sat down quickly. She broke out into a cold sweat and a sudden terrible realisation came upon her. The old lady pondered, "If the swine next door really was a doctor, and his name was Donovan… my God, what if he was the surgeon who had saved Belinda's life." The dates seemed to fit and there couldn't be that many people with the name Rick Donovan in the phone book. She remembered how he had pleaded with her to let him borrow the *Mini* in order to save the life of a sick person. What if that person had been her own Belinda? All her life Enid had considered herself an upright Christian woman. Could it be true that she had fought with a man who at the time was trying to save her own dear niece? The thought horrified her and she tried to dismiss it from her mind, especially if her dearest niece now had feelings for the fellow.

"Aunt Enid, are you sure you're OK?" Belinda asked.

"Well no actually I feel a bit light-headed; perhaps I've got a migraine coming on. Would you excuse me, dear?" The old lady did not wait for an answer. She headed out of the bedroom door, closing it carefully behind her, and then went downstairs with Molly in hot pursuit. Try as she might, Enid couldn't get Rick Donovan out of her mind. She needed to know the truth. She picked up the telephone in the hall and dialled the hospital.

"Oh, hello. Could you put me through to the gynaecology ward, please?" The switch board operator obliged and a kindly nurse picked up the receiver.

"Hello, this is the gynaecology ward, Sister Evans speaking, how can I help you?" A very proper and efficient sounding ward sister answered.

"Oh Hello…Sister Evans, this is Miss Jones speaking. You may remember my niece Belinda Jones was recently on the ward…"

"Yes of course I remember Belinda. How's she doing?"

"Very well thank you. I was after the name of the surgeon who was so wonderful to her. We thought we might send him a thank you card. Am I right in thinking it was a Mr Rawarse?" Enid tried to sound in control and confident, but inside she was shaking like a leaf.

"Yes Miss Jones, that's right, he was the consultant in charge, but Belinda was actually operated on by the senior registrar, Rick Donovan. Sir John Rawarse is away on sick leave at the moment."

"Oh my God," Enid whispered to herself as she nearly dropped the phone.

"Sorry Miss Jones, what did you say?"

"Oh… um… perhaps we'll send Mr Donovan a thank you card then," the old lady stuttered.

"Well there is no point in sending him a card here," the ward sister replied.

"Sorry? Why ever not?"

"Well, he's not coming to work at the moment." Sister Evans sounded a little sad.

"Oh I see, he's on holiday is he?"

"Well, not exactly Miss Jones." There was a pause in the conversation, almost as if the nursing sister was contemplating something, then her voice adopted a hushed conspiring tone. "Look, I shouldn't be telling you this, but he's been suspended. Can you believe it, the best gynaecologist we've got and the hospital management has suspended him."

"Oh, I am sorry to hear that dear, he was apparently an excellent doctor when caring for my Belinda. Whatever has he done?" Enid sounded as empathetic and understanding as possible, but secretly she was shaking with fear at the possibility of Rick Donovan being genuine.

"Look Miss Jones, I told you he was suspended because it might help his case if you write to the hospital saying how good Belinda's care was. I am afraid I really can't tell you why he was suspended, except to say that he is much respected by all his colleagues and is a very good and caring doctor. Furthermore there are rather bizarre and extenuating circumstances around the whole business but as far as I and my colleagues are concerned Mr Donovan acted with the best of intentions and ended up saving your Belinda's life." Sister Evans who was usually so prim and proper, a sort of by-the-book character, was being uncharacteristically open and frank.

Enid was shaking on the other end of the phone, "I quite understand dear, and of course I will write to the hospital authorities. I wonder, since he's not at the hospital, where shall I send this thank you card? I really would like to send him a token of our appreciation." The pensioner must have sounded extremely benign and indeed sincere, since the ward sister, disobeying all Trust instructions proceeded to give Rick's address over the phone. As she did so Enid gasped audibly as if she was stricken by some terrible pain. Her heart missed a beat and she felt it would almost stop. She felt sick and lightheaded, for Belinda's surgeon and her insufferable next door neighbour were one and the same.

Enid thanked Sister Evans in barely a whisper. She put the telephone down slowly and tried to compose herself. She sat down on a stool in the hall and buried her face in her hands. Molly, sensing that something was dreadfully wrong, whimpered quietly at her feet, nudging Enid delicately with her snout in a vain attempt to comfort her. "My God what have I done? I have so misjudged him," she whispered to herself. Enid now realised the gravity of her actions, behaviour that could possibly have resulted in Belinda's premature funeral. Furthermore Rick had been suspended from the hospital, presumably on the strength of the police charges made against him. And the only crime he committed was to save Belinda's life. What made her feel even worse, if that were possible, was that he had even tried to apologise with flowers for her and Doggie Chocs for Molly. Enid finally recognised that despite his obvious sincerity she had treated him with malice and sent him away, courtesy of Molly, with nothing but a sore bum. And that after he had saved the most important person in her life from the clutches of death. Even the police had informed her that Rick was a doctor, and on the night in question was on his way to save a patient. Little did Enid ever dream that the patient was her own dear niece. How selfish and proud she had been to continue to press charges. What sort of woman was she? Enid looked up from her defeated posture. "Come my girl, you must put things right. You must put things right straight away!" The old lady stood up determinedly and paced back and forth down the short hall as she thought of the best way to make amends. "What to do, what to do?" she chirped to herself.

Molly by now was looking thoroughly confused and started to whine. Enid comforted her, bending down and stroking her behind the ears. "It's all right my old thing, it's just your mum has got to do the right thing." Enid went back to the telephone, flipped through her address book and dialled the local police station.

"Hello, good morning. I'd like to speak to Sergeant Gary Dulwit please."

"Speaking." Sergeant Dulwit sounded fatigued on account of a rather amorous night with his beloved wife after heeding Mr Donovan's advice on HRT.

"Ah, Sergeant Dulwit, this is Miss Jones here. I'd like to drop all charges against Dr Donovan."

"Sorry, could you say that again?" Sergeant Dulwit

was more than slightly astonished and a touch confused. The ferocity of Enid's previous conviction that 'the bastard should go to jail' flooded back to him like a recurrent nightmare.

"Sergeant, are you deaf as well as dull? I'll say again for the benefit of your cloth ears... I'm dropping all charges against Dr Donovan."

"Um right you are Miss Jones. I see. Well actually I don't. Might I ask why the sudden change of heart?" Dulwit ventured and then wished he hadn't.

"I would have thought that is plainly obvious Sergeant Dulwit. A man like Dr Donovan deserves our thanks and I have no doubt he was acting in the best interest of his patients when he borrowed my car. I only wish to the good Lord above that you'd been clearer in your explanations regarding his conduct. This whole ridiculous situation could have been avoided. Now, good day to you." Enid put the phone down on the flabbergasted police officer.

She then picked up the receiver and dialled through to the hospital again. Someone on the other end answered.

"Hello, hospital switch board. How can I help you?"

"Hello. I'd like to speak to the hospital Chief

Executive please."

"I'm afraid that's not possible, I…"

"This is his wife speaking," Enid cut her off in midsentence. "And I don't want any messing around. This is a matter of the utmost urgency. Do you hear me?" Enid had no idea if the Chief Executive was male or female, but she knew the odds were in her favour. She also allowed herself a little white lie. It was after all in a good cause and she was sure that the Chief would not lower himself to speak to a little old pensioner, so her fib was justified.

"Err yes, madam, I'll put you through right away." The operator was not going to risk a slanging match with Mrs Harrington-Smythe. She put the call through direct to the Chief Executive's office. The telephone was answered by a rather posh, pompous-sounding male voice. It sounded as if its owner either had a plum in his mouth, or something stuck up his arse.

"Hello my darling plum-cake, what do I owe the unexpected pleasure of this call, were you missing your angel nana?" Harrington-Smythe smooched down the phone.

Enid had experienced some initial trepidation, but after hearing the CEO prattling on like a love sick twat, soon recovered her forthright manner.

"Certainly not!"

There followed a moment of embarrassed silence as the CEO tried in vain to make sense of his current predicament, "Oh...I...umm...err...Oh God, you are not the Press are you?" He was annoyed that he had been caught off guard.

Enid intervened, "No I am neither the Press, nor am I your darling plum-cake," Enid let the words 'darling plum-cake' hang for just a second or two. "My name is Miss Enid Jones and I am telephoning you to inform there has been a terrible mistake."

"Sorry, madam, but just who do you think you are and what on earth are you talking about?" Harrington-Smythe sounded irritated and his manner was condescending.

Immediately, Enid's hackles were up. "I told you, you rude man, my name is Miss Enid Jones and for your information my niece was recently admitted to your hospital." Enid tried to sound as haughty and plummy-voiced as possible. Her ploy seemed to work since Harrington-Smythe remained silent on the other end of the phone. She continued. "Mr Richard Donovan was the surgeon looking after my niece and I would like to say what an excellent job he did."

"Forgive me, but I don't understand quite what

the problem is." Harrington-Smythe sounded less officious and his previous condescending manner had disappeared.

"You've suspended him, that's the problem. A perfectly wonderful surgeon who saved my niece's life and you've bloody well suspended him." Enid was starting to enjoy herself. This pompous prat needed to be brought down a peg or two.

"I really don't know who you think you are but Mr Donovan's unfortunate circumstances have really got nothing to do with you. Now if you don't mind…" Harrington-Smythe tried to finish his sentence to no avail, Enid cut straight across the Chief Executive and left him hanging in mid-sentence.

"Excuse me but it has everything to do with me. You've suspended him for stealing my Mini on the night my niece, Miss Belinda Jones, was brought into your hospital. Now, I do not know what you are playing at, but Mr Donovan had my full permission to use my car and any question of him stealing it is absolutely outrageous. Do you hear me, Mr Harrington-Smythe or should I call you Angel Nana?"

"I… um…" the chief executive floundered on the other end of the phone, he was both embarrassed at his previous indiscretion and becoming less sure of himself. He certainly knew all about the Donovan case since he had ordered Andrew Kurfew, his favoured protégé, to do the dirty work and get rid of the surgeon. "But the police charges that were made…"

Enid struck whilst the iron was hot. "What police charges? I've spoken to Sergeant Dulwit himself. All police charges have been dropped since Mr Donovan was acting in an honourable fashion. Please feel free to telephone the police yourself. Thereafter, might I suggest that you or whoever it was that suspended Mr Donovan reverse that decision quickly or I will write to the Cardiff newspapers detailing how *you* in particular treat loyal staff. You never know the Press might also be interested in your rather bizarre telephone manner. Do I make myself clear, laddie?"

It irked Harrington-Smythe to be blackmailed and to be called 'laddie', as if he were a naughty boy, but Enid was evidently a worthy foe and all he needed was to be exposed in the local press as a doctor basher. The Chief Executive of the entire Health Board climbed down from his metaphorical lofty heights and gave in to the old age pensioner, becoming a slimy wimp in the process.

"Miss Jones, first of all let me say how grateful I am that you have brought this to my attention. If what you say is true - and I have no reason to doubt it," Harrington-Smythe quickly added, "then I shall have Mr Donovan reinstated at once. Furthermore you have my word as a gentleman that whoever dealt with this case will be reprimanded for their ineptness."

"Thank you for your understanding and prompt action. I have no doubt it will avert an ugly commotion with regard to our local newspapers, and only enhance your status as a fair and just manager. Now, good day to you, sir." Enid put the telephone down triumphantly.

In the meantime, Sir Archibald Harrington-Smythe was seething with rage at being spoken to in such a fashion and needed to release his pent up emotions on one of his unfortunate staff. He dialled Andrew Kurfew's telephone number. "Kurfew, is that you? This is the Chief Executive here."

"Oh, hello sir, how are you? Can I help you with anything? Anything at all, sir?" Kurfew grovelled to his boss. There was no doubt he was an expert bottom licker as well as thoroughly nasty piece of work.

"Yes, there is something you can do for me, first of all stop your obsequious grovelling and secondly reinstate Donovan immediately."

"But sir, the GMC, the police charges."

"I don't think you heard me Kurfew. All police charges have been dropped – there is no case against him so inform the GMC of *your* lamentable mistake and reinstate the bastard before I get hounded in the press as a medic basher......and Kurfew..."

"Yes Sir."

"Do it now!"

"Err... yes sir, of course sir."

CHAPTER 20

After her dear aunt had delivered breakfast on a tray and chatted briefly to her, Belinda couldn't help but wonder why Enid seemed flustered especially after Mr Donovan's name was mentioned. Enid had rushed off down stairs and appeared to be making all sorts of phone calls in a rather frantic, but hushed manner.

The young woman sighed, reached for the local newspaper so eloquently delivered by Molly and opened the Daily Rag on the second page. Her eyes remained fixed on an article entitled, 'Brilliant Gynaecologist Suspended Following Heroic Action'. The look on Belinda's face was one of complete disbelief. She held her breath as she read on, realising that she was a major player in the story and how the unselfish and radical action of Dr Rick Donovan had prevented her ending up in the mortuary. The newspaper account was written by a well-known local journalist, Geoff Woodruff. He described how he had first met Rick Donovan on a Cardiff bus. On the public transport he had witnessed Dr Donovan saving the life of a drunken youth by stopping him choking to death on his own vomit. Apparently Rick had been covered from head to foot with green, foul-smelling puke courtesy of the inebriated youth. Yet even then, the noble doctor had performed mouth to mouth resuscitation. The boy's parents had been contacted and were full of praise for the magnanimous medic. What was even more extraordinary was that despite his heroic life-saving antics, Dr Donovan had been suspended from working as a doctor that very same day.

The newspaper article went on to describe the events leading up to Rick's suspension and how in another life-saving episode prior to the vomiting youth, there had been mayhem in the receiving A&E Department when a young girl had arrived through the doors, close to death. The paper reported the somewhat difficult acquisition of a marvellous old *Austin Mini* to transport the life-saving medic up to the hospital and then how another life was saved. Although no other names were disclosed probably for legal reasons, there was no doubt who the main characters were and it was clear to Belinda that her aunt had not only obstructed Rick from rushing to save her life, but she had then insisted on pressing charges, resulting in his suspension.

The journalist revealed his sources to be the well-respected ambulance paramedics Paddy O'Connell and Horace Finnigan. Belinda recognised their names and remembered them when they visited her as she recovered in hospital. She knew too that they were instrumental in saving her life. Belinda put the paper down and just stared at the opposite wall in a state of shock. She truly could not believe the things that she had just read. The sound of the front door opening and closing roused her from her trance-like disposition, her aunt had evidently nipped out for a while. She placed the tray to one side and carefully got up out of bed, being careful to hold her wound as she did so. She then dressed as quickly as her predicament would allow and packed a small bag of her belongings before telephoning for a taxi on the upstairs extension. She knew she couldn't stay with her aunt, feeling as she did, she just had to get out. She made her way gingerly down the stairs to find Molly sitting in the hall whimpering quietly by the front door, it was most unlike her Aunt Enid to go anywhere without her pooch. This was all very odd. Belinda wrote a note on the pad by the telephone, thanking her aunt for allowing her to stay, but that under the circumstances she felt happier going back to her own flat. She didn't really know what else to write. She only knew that she was appalled by what she had read, felt hurt that Enid had acted in such a manner, and to top it all felt awful that Rick's career was now in jeopardy.

Instead of signing the note, 'With much love' as she usually did, Belinda merely signed her name. She then waited by the window in the front room for the ordered taxi. She dreaded the old lady returning before she left, but thankfully the taxi was prompt. Belinda patted Molly affectionately.

"I'm sorry old girl but I've just got to go. Goodbye, and look after Aunt Enid for me." She was almost in tears as she climbed carefully into the taxi. She could see Molly's little face in the front window looking morose and down hearted. The driver started his car, crunched the gearbox into first and Belinda was gone.

Having sorted out Rick's reinstatement with regard to his medical career, and having ensured that all police charges had been dropped, Enid couldn't help feeling reasonably pleased with herself. The success she'd achieved in completing these tasks gave her the confidence to tackle the last and most difficult of scenarios - that of saying sorry to Rick Donovan face to face. She knew that now was as good a time as any, and that delaying would only make the situation more difficult. In any case, how could she possibly face her niece again without at least doing all in her power to make amends with the person who had saved Belinda's life?

Enid decided to take the bull by the horns. While Belinda was eating her breakfast in bed, she had strode determinedly out of the front door of her little terraced house, ensuring that Molly stayed behind, pushed open Rick's front gate and walked up the short path. The pensioner had stood at his front door for some moments, trying to summon up courage. Then with more than a little trepidation, Enid had knocked on her neighbour's front door. She waited thirty seconds or so. There was no answer. She knocked again, still no answer. She knocked a third time, and on this occasion there were some stirrings from within the little house. Enid had waited patiently and eventually her persistence paid off, but she was ill prepared for what greeted her.

Rick stood with the front door half-open, he looked terrible. His eyes were sunk deep into their sockets and enormous black bags hung down from them; it looked as if he had been weeping. His skin was pale and lacklustre, and his hair dirty and dishevelled. He wore a torn, grimy dressing gown and certainly looked as if he had had little or no sleep. To make matters worse he smelt of alcohol and it was still only mid-morning.

As she stood facing her previous arch enemy, Enid thought to herself, 'Oh my God, what have I done to this boy?' and her maternal instincts took over.

"Dr Donovan," she felt addressing him by his proper title was appropriate to let Rick know that she acknowledged that he was a real doctor. Yet in his catatonic stupor, Rick hardly responded and the old lady's heart went out to him. She was surprised that he had even made it to the door. "Rick," she gently voiced. "I'm so very sorry, I didn't realise who you were and I have wronged you. Please forgive me."

Enid wanted to tell him that she'd fixed everything with regard to the police and the hospital and that there was nothing more to worry about, but he didn't seem to be taking anything in. The gynaecologist seemed to smile almost as if through a hazy fog. He didn't reply with a triumphant 'I told you so', and his smile wasn't derisive, it was genuine.

Rick whispered, "Enid love, it's all right and thank

you for coming over," as if he were the one trying to comfort her. Through the alcoholic mist she saw no malice as she had always thought, but a good man, albeit one who was having a rough time at the moment. Enid sensed something else was amiss. Rick Donovan's appearance and sense of loss reminded her of someone grieving for the death of someone dear to them. Enid sensed his suffering beyond the debacle that she was responsible for and she wanted to help him so very badly.

"Oh Rick, it's far from alright, look at you. Please let me come in, I must try and sort out the mess that I've caused," and with that she pushed forward. Rick capitulated easily, he was in no fit state to resist and before he knew it the pensioner was inside his house. Enid looked around inquisitively and noted to her surprise that the little house was tastefully decorated and comfortable, but what a mess. Dirty washing up lay strewn about the place, the carpets had probably not seen daylight on account of rubbish strewn about the place, and the smell of alcohol emanated from the empty bottles of spirits scattered across the coffee table. Rick collapsed in an armchair and in a state of complete ambivalence his heavy eyelids closed and within minutes he was fast asleep. Enid rolled up her sleeves and started tidying up the place. It was the only way she knew of to make amends. She found some dustbin bags in the kitchen and began to clear the rubbish from the main living room. Underneath the empty bottles of booze on the coffee table, she thought she found the reason for Rick's distress. It was an open letter. Enid tried to avoid reading the cursed piece of paper but in the end her inquisitiveness got the better of her. When she put the letter down, she found herself moved to tears. A person called 'Cissy' had been killed in a road traffic accident two days ago. Enid had no idea who 'Cissy' was but could only assume that it was someone of great importance to Rick, perhaps his sister or even his mother. Little wonder then that he had turned to drink. The old woman scrubbed, mopped, swept and hoovered her way around the little terrace house. She changed the linen, washed up, and put on two loads of washing. It was mid-afternoon when she had finished.

To his enormous surprise, the old lady forced Rick to drink plenty of black coffee and fussed around him like an old mother hen. Rick by now had come around to some semblance of normal consciousness and looked about in a confused manner.

"Enid, what are you doing? I thought you hated me."

"Well Doctor, it just shows how wrong you can be about people. I made a huge mistake in misjudging you and now I just want to make amends, if you'll allow me." There was period of silence before Enid spoke again.

"You haven't had anything decent to eat for a while, have you?"

"Well, um, no… I guess not." Rick was flabbergasted.

"In that case, I shall go next door and make you a nice steak and kidney pie. May I suggest that you have a wash and shave beforehand? I will be about an hour."

Rick felt strangely reassured by his neighbour's kind but forthright manner. Probably because he knew that two days was long enough to spend in an alcoholic stupor, and no matter what tragedy had passed he would sooner or later have to face the world again. Enid was inferring that he needed to get a grip. The old girl was right. Enid left him in charge of his sparklingly clean house and returned next door. As she walked through her own front door Molly scampered joyfully up to her. She leant over and patted the mongrel before calling up the stairs, "Belinda dear, you must forgive me. I got rather waylaid."

There was no response. The old lady called again. Still there was no reply. Enid wearily trudged up the stairs; she was tired from her efforts of the morning. "Tut! Tut! Fallen asleep again, my dear. I am sorry it's so late, I'll get you some lunch now." When she arrived in the spare room, it was of course devoid of any human life and stranger still, the bed was made and Belinda's personal belongings had disappeared. The morning newspaper was folded neatly on the bed. Enid picked it up in order to take it downstairs and she gasped as read the title of the headline facing her, 'Brilliant Gynaecologist Suspended Following Heroic Action'. She resignedly sat down on the bed and read the article from beginning to end. It really did make her out to be an old dragon and on reflection Enid thought that perhaps anyone reading it was entitled to that view.

"So now my sweet niece, you also know what a bitch I have been. No wonder you've gone." The pensioner sadly trudged down the stairs and found Belinda's note on the telephone pad. She sat on the bottom step and wept. Molly was by now feeling somewhat insecure and joined her mistress with a morose howl of her own. It was not long before the tears stopped. Enid regained her determination to put things right, so she dried her tears, and then picking up the telephone dialled Belinda's number.

"Hello, this is Belinda Jones."

"Belinda dear, before you put the phone down on your old aunt please hear me out." There was an ominous silence on the other end of the telephone. Enid took a big breath and continued. "I know I have done wrong and there are no excuses…but please forgive a foolish old woman. I couldn't bear to lose you… Belinda?" There was a further period of silence. "I've tried to make things right with the hospital and the Police, and this morning I've been to see Dr Donovan to say how very sorry I am. He is very fragile at the moment, as well as everything I've put him through I think one of his close relatives died two days ago in a road traffic accident. He needs help and support…"

Belinda interrupted. "He saved my life, Aunt Enid. I know that this sounds a bit weird…but I have feelings for him… I must go and see him, it's the least I can do." The telephone line went dead.

Enid sighed and put the phone down. She thought about telephoning Belinda back and volunteering to go and fetch her in her *Mini*, but knew her niece was single minded now and would phone for a taxi. Going into automatic mode, the pensioner went into her kitchen and started preparing a meal for her next door neighbour. Anticipating her niece's arrival next door, she made enough steak and kidney pie for two and then added an array of vegetables and a couple of Yorkshire puddings. She covered the two plates with cling film and put them on a tray and then added two bowls of strawberries and cream for dessert, as well two glasses and a bottle of flavoured water. Enid left the prepared food in the kitchen and went into the hall. She took the spare key to the *Mini* off a hook and slipped it into an envelope with a little note that read:

Dear Rick,

Please forgive a foolish old lady.

If you ever have an emergency again you have your own key. It's the spare to the Mini.

I am truly sorry.

From the old bat next door

Enid

The old woman collected the tray from the kitchen, placed the envelope addressed to 'Dr Rick Donovan' so that it leaned against the bottled water and took the meals next door.

CHAPTER 21

Rick stood in the shower wallowing in the streaming water that imparted a freshness and vitality to his abused body. He felt somewhat bewildered that his witch of a next door neighbour had been so pleasant to him. As he stepped out of the shower and wrapped himself in a freshly laundered towel, the telephone rang. Thanks to Enid he was sufficiently sober to speak coherently.

"Hello, this is Rick Donovan."

"Dr Donovan, good afternoon. This is Sergeant Dulwit from the local police station."

Rick remained silent on the other end of the phone, and the sergeant continued.

"I know this may come as a bit of a shock, but I am sir, very pleased to inform you that all charges against you concerning the theft of Miss Enid Jones's *Mini* have been dropped."

"I beg your pardon, can you say that again?" Rick replied, not believing his own ears.

"Certainly sir, the charges against you have been dropped. For some extraordinary reason Miss Jones telephoned the station this morning and dropped all charges. We have yet to receive written confirmation, but I feel confident that you are in the clear."

"Well I'll be damned."

"My sentiments entirely sir; it would appear that in the eyes of Miss Jones you have gone from being public enemy number one to Mother Teresa on steroids. Even stranger sir, she spoke about you as if you were her long lost son awaiting canonisation. Derogatory terms such as 'scumbag' and 'bastard' have been thoroughly eradicated from her vocabulary. I have no explanation sir. I am lost for words. However, I thought you would want to know sooner rather than later."

"Indeed Sergeant Dulwit, and many thanks for the good news."

"By the way, Doctor, I heeded your advice, you know about the HRT for the wife, and our GP has put her on the patches. Well we've never had it so good. It's like being newly-weds all over again!"

"Golly....um, I'm very pleased to hear it Sergeant

Dulwit. Now if you'll forgive me, I must go, thank you for the news… bye." Rick had no desire to hear any further details on Sergeant Dulwit's rekindled love life and quickly put the telephone down. No sooner had he done so than it rang again.

"Bloody 'ell, what's going on?" Rick picked the receiver up, "Hello."

"Um, hello, is that Dr Donovan?"

"Yes that's right." Rick recognised the voice on the other end of the phone, but it sounded muffled and timid, as if the person concerned was trying to conceal his identity.

"I am phoning on behalf of your hospital management," the disguised voice continued. "Dr Donovan, we have reviewed your case at the highest level and in view of the extenuating circumstances surrounding the theft of Miss Jones's car and indeed your own excellent record at this hospital…" There was an audible strain at the other end of the phone almost as if it hurt to say it. "We have decided to reinstate you forthwith."

Rick was dumbfounded and then angry. "Bloody hell, suspend, reinstate, suspend, reinstate. Who's running the bloody Trust? A sodding jack-in-the-box? Do you guys know your arse from your elbow or have you all just got shit for brains?"

"Look, just be grateful you are not suspended all right." The strange voice became clearer and was tinged with irritation.

"I know that voice. It's the delightful Mr Kurfew isn't it? Well, well, how decent of you to sort things out and all for my good eh? So what happened to make you change your mind Kurfew? Are more staff off with the flu or did your conscience get the better of you? No, I forgot you haven't got a conscience have you?"

"If you must know the chief exec merely reviewed your case and decided to give you a reprieve. Now if you're unhappy with that I can soon let him know."

But Rick knew that something was up. The management had obviously been scared into reinstating him, but why? Police charges had been dropped that day and Enid had been responsible for that. "I don't suppose this has got anything to do with the police dropping all charges has it?" Rick baited the hospital manager. There was an embarrassed silence on the other end of the telephone. Rick continued. "And I bet the police didn't ring you, why would they?" There was a further pause. "Bloody hell, Enid rang you didn't she? I bet she telephoned the bloody Chief Executive of the Hospital Board."

There was a further period of silence that confirmed Rick's suspicions. "She did ring him and no doubt scared him shitless and now he's getting you to do the dirty work." Rick could almost hear Kurfew whimper. "Well thank you so much Kurfew, that must have been hard having to phone and let me know the good news," Rick ended sarcastically.

"A lot bloody harder than you think," Kurfew whispered.

"Be a good chap and sort out the paperwork, OK? Then you can get back to tunnelling up the chief exec's backside. Goodbye." Rick put the telephone down triumphantly. "Enid old girl, I think I am starting to like you."

The doorbell rang. A contrite old age pensioner stood at Rick Donovan's front door with a peace offering. Her wig was slightly dishevelled, and her mascara was blotched around her swollen eyes. It was Rick's turn to be taken aback; the old lady had obviously been crying. She quickly handed him the tray and with a whisper of, "Sorry Rick, forgive me," turned and fled back into her own house. Rick half opened his mouth to say thank you, not only for the food and sorting him out earlier, but for dropping all the charges and then for giving the hospital management a run for their money. But she was too quick and before he could get the words out she was gone. He spoke the words out loud anyway then thoughtfully closed the front door. He took the tray through to the lounge and only then noticed it had been set for two. Before he had time to think about the duplication, the doorbell sounded again.

"God, it's like bloody Euston Station," he muttered as he opened the front door. When he saw her standing there in front of him, Rick Donovan was almost speechless. His heart fluttered as his spirits soared and all the trauma of the past few days evaporated into nothingness, rendered irrelevant by her presence.

The two of them stood motionless and unsure until finally Belinda broke the silence. "Rick... oh... may I call you Rick?"

"Yes of course, Belinda," the gynaecologist stood dumbstruck at his front door.

"Rick... umm... may I come in?" Her voice was sweet as honey dew, and clear as a mountain stream. She smiled at him as she spoke and he felt his heart would burst.

"Oh... so sorry, yes of course, come in," he

stuttered awkwardly, afraid to reveal the true depth of feeling he had for her. It was Belinda who once again took the initiative. She looked at him with those piercing green eyes, took hold of his hands and gently pulled him towards her. They held each other on the front door step of the little two-up, two-down terraced house in Cardiff and each of them knew the depth of feeling they had for each other. Rick took care to be so gentle, she had only recently had surgery, but Belinda did not hold back and her embrace was surprisingly powerful.

As she held him, Belinda whispered, "God, I've been wanting to do this since the first time I saw you."

"Well, I have to say that the thought did cross my mind too!" Rick grinned at the beautiful young woman in front of him.

Enid watched them momentarily from her bay window and then feeling almost as if she was invading their privacy turned away. A single tear trickled down the old lady's cheek, but inside she was smiling and much relieved in the knowledge that she had managed to put things right.

That afternoon the couple shared many things that neither had ever spoken of to others. They took turns to listen and then to speak. They ate the meal Enid had affectionately prepared for them and chatted long into the evening and then the night, getting to know to each other better. Wounds were healed and misunderstandings were rectified. It turned out that 'Cissy' was the Donovan family cat, much beloved by Rick's mother. Mrs Donovan had been so bereft that she had sent recorded delivery letters to all immediate family and friends, informing them of her pussy's demise. The unfortunate cat had been run over by Rick's father after he was forced to share the marital bed with it and his cat-loving wife. Apparently the feline departure had been an accident, although Rick had his suspicions. He was reasonably sure that his father, fed up with the competition and wanting some private pussy of his own had murdered the unlucky moggie.

Belinda laughed heartily when she realised that it was the undoing of a family cat that had brought her and Rick together. Sometime later, Rick opened the envelope Enid had put on the tray and took out the key to the *Mini*, with the note she had written. He chuckled to himself as he read the note. "She really is an old sweetheart, look, read this." Rick handed the piece of paper to Belinda, who read it and smiled fondly. Rick had already told Belinda about the events of the day and how Enid had been busy telephoning both the Police and the hospital management.

"I think my Aunt Enid has learnt her lesson. I ought to pop in and see her, to sort things out."

"Well, she's got my vote. It must have taken a lot of courage to do what she did today and I have to say she looked pretty upset when she dropped the tray of grub around." The couple agreed that they would have to make amends with Enid and put the old girl out of her misery. When it was time for Belinda to leave, Rick found he was hopelessly nervous, summoning up the courage to kiss her. She laughed, not out of mockery but out of joy, and, holding his face in her hands, tenderly kissed him. She tasted exquisite as of the finest of wines and her sensuality was almost overpowering. He was reluctant to let her go, but knew that he must respect her wishes.

"Rick, I don't know quite how to say this, but I feel like I have known you all my life." Belinda spoke the words with such conviction and fondness that Rick could only envisage a future of joy and hopefully sensuous pleasure. She looked once more into his eyes and was gone.

Enid had two visitors that evening, the first of whom was her beloved niece. Aunt and niece hugged each other and Enid couldn't stop the tears from falling, such was her relief. Kind words, forgiving words were spoken and reconciliation took place. Molly was especially pleased to see the mood change in her mistress even after Belinda had returned to her own apartment. The next visitor was a Dr Rick Donovan who stood outside her house with a bunch of flowers and an inane grin on his face. Despite the fact that it was a quarter to midnight, Enid was delighted. However, as the door was opened Molly flew out, unaware of the change in circumstances that dictated a more amicable arrangement. Her teeth were bared and she snarled viciously, and as she travelled forward at an alarming speed, her beady eyes focused on Rick..

"Molly, stop!" Enid screamed as if her very life depended on it. "Naughty girl! That is no way to treat a friend." The little dog obediently ceased her charge and was only inches from Rick's dangling testicles when she turned and scampered back into the house, somewhat confused.

"Oh Rick, um, Dr Donovan, I am sorry. Please forgive my little dog's indiscretion," Enid muttered apologetically, looking down to avert his gaze.

"Please Enid, um Miss Jones, think nothing of it.

After all we haven't been the best of neighbours to each other recently and certainly I am to blame as much as anyone."

"Nonsense, it's my fault for being a stubborn, selfish old woman and I hope you can find it in your heart to forgive me for being so foolish."

"Enid, please, let's not argue over whose fault it is. I just came over tonight to say thank you for today. You've been fantastic. A single day and you've turned my whole life around. I've even been reinstated at the hospital."

"Quite right, too. I hear you are an excellent doctor and you saved my Belinda's life - no thanks to me." Enid again looked remorseful, so Rick changed tack.

"I hear you gave those idiots called managers a good talking to. You know, up at the hospital."

"Rick, you've no idea - that Mr Harrington-what's-his-name, what a pompous twit..." Rick let the old lady expand on her conversation with the Chief Executive and chuckled to himself as the story unfolded, with particular reference to 'Plum-cake' and 'Darling nana' . Having found a common enemy, the two of them continued the conversation in Enid's drawing room. The old girl got out the sweet sherry, and reluctant as he was Rick found himself accepting a glass. Molly, content that the bastard next door was a foe turned friend, happily nuzzled at his feet and was further wooed by the intermittent *Walkers* crisp that Rick dropped in her direction. The night ended when Rick accepted an invitation to Sunday lunch, after reassurance from Enid that Belinda would be there. At her front door, much to Rick's surprise, Enid bid her next door neighbour goodnight by embracing him as she would have her own son.

Rick returned to work at the hospital a few days later after written confirmation of the cessation of his suspension. He had mixed feelings as he walked through the main hospital doors and made his way up to the Department of Obstetrics and Gynaecology. He peeped tentatively through the glass panels of the heavy fire doors that opened onto the gynaecology ward - it all seemed quiet enough. He pushed the doors open and strode onto the ward. Rick couldn't put his finger on it, but he sensed that something was not quite right. The ward was too quiet, there were no nurses to be seen. Even the ward receptionist was absent from her place of duty. The gynaecologist rounded the corner into the staff coffee room and then stood agog at what lay before him. A huge banner hung across the room and read, 'Welcome Back Rick'. A throng of staff, including nursing staff, doctors, medics and even the cleaners applauded him and then Horace and Paddy led a round of, "Three cheers for Rick", which was quickly followed by a chorus of "For he's a jolly good fellow".

Dr Rick Donovan shook hands and embraced his friends and colleagues and was quite overwhelmed by his welcome back. Horace stood up and gave a short impromptu speech to which Rick replied, thanking everyone for their support. Just before the small crowd dispersed and went back to their respective duties, the joviality of the occasion was thwarted. The gaunt frame of Sir John Rawarse appeared through the door and the gathering was plunged into a deathly silence. Even Paddy and Horace went quiet. Sir John Rawarse slowly walked into the room and ignoring everyone else walked up to Rick. His voice had not lost its previous authority.

"Mr Donovan, I suppose 'a welcome back' is in order."

"Thank you Sir John," Rick replied and everyone in the room relaxed just a little.

Then Rawarse, looking his foreboding best added, "A word in private if you please. I'll see you in my office in two minutes," and with that Sir John stomped out. Following Rawarse's exit, the room slowly came back to life and everyone looked suitably sorry for Rick. For his part, the gynaecologist again thanked everyone and made his way up to his boss's office. He knocked twice on the door and then waited.

"Enter!" Sir John bellowed from behind his desk and Rick hesitantly proceeded into the room.

"Now young Donovan, I have two things I wish you to be aware of. The first is that I do not approve of parties on the gynaecology ward. This morning's little escapade was on NHS property and in NHS time. We are paid to treat patients on the ward, Mr Donovan, not to host reception parties, even if it was to welcome you back." Sir John cleared his throat. He was obviously not finding this as easy as he normally did. "However, on this occasion I will overlook this indiscretion since I am aware that you knew nothing about it. But please ensure such festivities are not repeated. Do I make myself clear?" Rawarse fixed Rick with a characteristically menacing glare.

"Um, yes Sir."

"Good. Now, to proceed with other matters. The past few weeks I believe have represented a difficult time in your life." And now as he spoke Sir John Rawarse looked straight ahead, gazing into some distant horizon. "Certainly the events of the recent past have given me a new perspective on life." The old man paused thoughtfully before continuing on. "I am told, Mr Donovan, that you have run my firm both efficiently and competently in my absence, despite the best efforts of the management to thwart you. Of course, I would expect no less from my senior registrar. But I also owe you my personal thanks for aiding and abetting a cantankerous old surgeon's recovery."

"Err, right sir, thank you sir." The old man cleared his throat again.

"There are two other matters I wish to discuss with you."

"Yes, Sir John?"

"As you know all too well, I have been unwell and in fact am only here today to collect a few papers before returning home to continue my rehabilitation. I require my senior registrar to take over many of my duties while I recuperate. Thereafter, I believe that next month the department will be advertising for a new consultant. I want you to apply for the position. Strictly between the two of us, I believe you would stand a very good chance of being appointed. *When* you are appointed I would require you to take over a number of my patients as I near retirement. Do you understand, Mr Donovan?"

"Yes, of course sir."

"There is one particular patient whom I believe even the psychiatrists have refused to treat - a woman with Spontaneous Orgasm Syndrome. It is unseemly for the senior consultant of the department to be exposed to such patients in his outpatient clinic, especially when their orgasms are so vocal."

"No sir, that wouldn't do at all. I would be happy to take over her care." Rick laughed internally but remained straight-faced and serious externally.

"Excellent. You may go now." Sir John dismissed his junior colleague. As Rick exited through the door, Sir John Rawarse spoke again and there was a genuine smile on his face. "Rick, one more thing."

"Yes sir?"

"Good to have you back."

Rick turned to his boss. "Good to be back sir."

GLOSSARY OF TERMS

CCU – coronary care unit

Decompensating – deteriorating so that death is near

Defibrillate – to shock the heart into restarting

Ectopic pregnancy – pregnancy outside the womb

Exsanguinate – bleed to death

Extubate – to remove a tube from the windpipe

Heimlich manoeuvre – procedure that involves standing behind a person with arms placed around them and hands linked thrusting inwards and upwards with the aim of displacing an object stuck in their windpipe

ICU – Intensive Care Unit

Intubate – to pass a tube into the windpipe

O neg – stands for 'O' negative blood; can be given whatever the blood group of the patient in an emergency

Pulse oximeter – instrument that reads levels of oxygen in the blood

Sats – saturation of blood with oxygen; levels of oxygen in the body.

ABOUT THE AUTHOR

Born in South Africa, educated in England and Wales, and now living in God's own Country of Wales with his family, Sean was previously a Squadron Leader in the RAF and a GP, before retraining as a Consultant Obstetrician and Gynaecologist serving the people of the South Wales Valleys.

Sean has been a doctor for almost 30 years and his experience varies from helping out those less fortunate than us in Uganda, to facilitating IVF treatments for infertile couples.

Medics, Minis and Mayhem (amended from a previous work "Diary of a Gynaecologist" which was published under a pseudonym), is the prequel to another fictional piece of work, "Hospital Blues". Sean has also published Infertility, IVF and Miscarriage, a self-help book for the general public, to give guidance to the 1 in 6 couples unable have their own children and is in the process of publishing a number of fun children's rhyming books.

He lives in Cardiff with his wife, three children and a golden Labrador called Beano.

Printed in Poland
by Amazon Fulfillment
Poland Sp. z o.o., Wrocław

51431774R00163